'Even you cannot de̶̶̶ ̶ our child wo̶̶̶ ̶̶̶̶ rom having ̶̶̶̶ ̶ are married t̶̶

Her brow plea̶̶̶ ̶̶ confusion. 'Run that by me again…married to each other?'

Brilliant dark eyes flashed gold over her. Cristos flung his arms wide in a volatile gesture of expressive frustration. 'Obviously we're going to have to get married!'

'Oh, no, we're not… Go lay your sacrificial head on someone else's block!' Betsy advised, fighting to keep the lid on her absolute astonishment that he should even consider offering matrimony. 'I want to do the best I can for our baby as well, but wild horses wouldn't get me to the altar with a guy like you!'

'What do you mean—a guy like me?' Cristos demanded. 'I will be an excellent husband and father.'

Betsy tilted up her chin. 'But you won't be *my* husband.'

In the silence that spread like an oil slick waiting for a torch to ignite it, a manservant crept in to announce that lunch was being served.

Lynne Graham was born in Northern Ireland and has been a keen Mills & Boon® reader since her teens. She is very happily married, with an understanding husband who has learned to cook since she started to write! Her five children keep her on her toes. She has a very large dog, which knocks everything over, a very small terrier, which barks a lot, and two cats. When time allows, Lynne is a keen gardener.

Recent titles by the same author:

BRIDES OF L'AMOUR

THE FRENCHMAN'S LOVE-CHILD
THE ITALIAN BOSS'S MISTRESS
THE BANKER'S CONVENIENT WIFE

THE STEPHANIDES PREGNANCY

BY
LYNNE GRAHAM

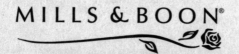

*First published in Great Britain 2004
Harlequin Mills & Boon Limited,
Eton House, 18-24 Paradise Road, Richmond, Surrey TW9 1SR*

© Lynne Graham 2004

ISBN 0 263 83735 1

*Set in Times Roman 10½ on 12 pt.
01-0504-47844*

*Printed and bound in Spain
by Litografia Rosés, S.A., Barcelona*

CHAPTER ONE

CHRISTOS STEPHANIDES had never been into women in uniform. Had he been, the world would certainly have known about it for the tabloid press reported his every move. A startlingly handsome Greek tycoon with a legendary appetite for super fast cars, luxury homes and dazzlingly beautiful women, Cristos was hotter than hot in the gossip columns.

The young woman who had caught his attention, however, was not in his usual style. Nor was she even aware of his scrutiny because the tinted windows on his limousine shielded him from view. Tall and slender, she wore a dark green fitted jacket and tailored skirt that accentuated her tiny waist and delicate curves just as her plain shoes showed off her award-worthy legs.

'That woman in the peaked cap. Is that an army uniform?' Cristos enquired idly of his second cousin, Spyros Zolottas.

The portly older man peered out. 'She looks more like a flight attendant.'

At the exact moment that Cristos was about to look away, a gust of wind dislodged the woman's cap and sent it careening along the ground. Vibrant streamers of Titian hair flew out in an arc behind her as she sprinted off in pursuit. She caught up with the cap only a few feet from his car. Spring sunshine flamed over the glorious hair she was struggling to coil back into concealment. Surprised by the vivid beauty of her oval face, Cristos stared. Luminous eyes and a luscious cherry-pink mouth highlighted skin as fine and smooth as alabaster: she was knock-down stunning.

Timon, his PA, said quietly, 'I think she might be a chauffeur.'

Disconcertion pleated Cristos' ebony brows, for to his mind a chauffeur fell into the same prohibited category as a servant. Watching the redhead climb into the driving seat of a Bentley that bore the discreet but unmistakable logo of a hire company on the rear bumper, he quirked an ebony brow. 'A strange choice of career for a woman.'

Predictably, Spyros loosed a sleazy snigger. 'With a body like that she may well find it very lucrative.'

Distaste filled Cristos. Spyros had always given him the creeps but he was family and Cristos had been raised to rate blood ties higher than other more instinctive responses.

'Are you thinking of your betrothed?' Having mistaken the reason for the younger man's silence, Spyros released another suggestive laugh. 'Petrina is a well-brought-up girl who knows her place, and if she doesn't know it yet you're just the man to tell her!'

'We will not discuss my engagement,' Cristos murmured, his dark, deep drawl sounding a cool note of warning, which in no way reflected the level of his exasperation.

Cristos was a Stephanides and Petrina was a Rhodias. Their families had long been linked in business and marriage would forge even closer ties. Matrimony was for the preservation of wealth and power and the raising of the next generation. Nobody expected Cristos to be faithful but it would be tasteless to acknowledge that fact out loud. His cousin's vulgarity offended him.

In truth, Cristos had no time for the other man's laboured efforts to flatter and amuse him because he was already waiting for the usual punchline to come. After all, Spyros only ever approached him when he wanted money. Once Spyros had concocted elaborate tales of investments gone wrong and sure-fire business ventures that required capital. If those failed to impress, he would then turn the sob story screws by talking about how his family would suffer for his 'misfortunes'. A gambler and a waster, Spyros had once revelled in his reputation of never having had to work a day in his forty-odd years of life.

Six months ago, Cristos had destroyed the legend by putting Spyros to work in the London office of a freight company, one of the many subsidiary businesses that made up the vast Stephanides empire. He had hoped that, separated from familiar haunts and cronies, Spyros would make a fresh start. To aid that objective, Cristos had paid off all his cousin's debts. His own grandfather, Patras, had laughed like a hyena. In fact, when Cristos had given Spyros a job Patras had laughed so hard he had almost needed resuscitation.

'Spyros is a leech and a loser. There's one in every family and we're too rich to let his nearest and dearest starve. Pay him to keep him out of our hair. You won't change him.' Patras had laid a bet that within months Spyros would have reverted to his old habits.

Cristos had accepted the bet. He saw no reason why the Stephanides clan should fund the dissolute lifestyle that shamed and distressed Spyros' wife and daughters. Although he had every respect for his grandfather, it was his firm belief that someone should have made Spyros toe the line a long time ago. Now Cristos believed that he had lost that bet, for his keenly intelligent gaze had already noted that his late mother's cousin was betraying all the visible stress of a man striving to rise to the challenge of an awkward occasion.

'I know you have to be wondering why I came to meet you off your plane.' Spyros paused and breathed in deep. 'I wanted to thank you personally for the opportunity you gave me last year to turn my life around.'

Lean, strong face expressionless, Cristos stared steadily back at the older man, his surprise that his cousin should speak so freely in front of Timon concealed. 'If that has been the result, I am happy for you,' he murmured with his slow, devastating smile.

Cristos was enough of a cynic to be disconcerted but he was also genuinely pleased.

'You will join us for dinner this evening before you leave?' Spyros pressed with enthusiasm.

Cristos had had other plans. His current mistress would be waiting at the apartment. The perfect end to a long day of business meetings was sex on silk sheets with a woman who would meet his every expectation with unquestioning zeal. With regret he shelved that sensual image and cursed his powerful libido. His principles had spoken: the very least that Spyros deserved was recognition of his achievement.

Before she had even arrived at Gemma and Rory's apartment in the leafy city suburbs, Betsy had promised herself that she would not be over-sensitive to anything her sister said.

So when Gemma widened her china-blue eyes and tossed her pale blonde head and said, 'I think being very skinny is aging,' Betsy, who stuffed herself with biscuits in the forlorn hope that she would develop a larger bosom, just smiled and said nothing.

When Gemma exclaimed in horror over the nails that Betsy had broken tinkering with a temperamental car engine, Betsy said nothing and hid her hands below the table as much as she could. In the same way, she withstood the suggestion that her casual jeans and shirt made her look like a boy and even a later reference to her lack of material success in the world. Indeed she was proud of herself for not rising to the bait.

Rory shared the same table, both with them and not with them, his discomfiture at the atmosphere between his girlfriend and her older sister pronounced. Every so often he made a clumsy attempt to bring in a new conversational subject but no matter what it was it always seemed to provide Gemma with more grist for her mill. Betsy studied Rory in a quick stolen glance. He looked grim, tense and embarrassed. Like Betsy, he was in the dark as to why Gemma seemed to have a need to verbally attack Betsy in every way she could.

After all, on the face of things, Betsy rather than Gemma should have been the sister with the axe to grind and the chip on her shoulder. Three years earlier, Betsy and Rory had been on the brink of getting engaged when Gemma had announced that she was pregnant and that Rory was the father of the baby she was carrying. Their parents had urged Betsy to take the news on the chin. She had done so. She had been far too proud to show any sign of wanting to hang onto a man who had gone behind her back to sleep with her very much prettier sister. She had also cared too much for both Rory and Gemma to have made a truly ghastly situation worse than it already had been and tear her whole family apart. And unhappily for her, Betsy reflected ruefully, she had never yet learned how *not* to love Rory.

'Every other single girl I know is out partying seven nights a week…I can't believe that you *still* haven't found a bloke of your own!' Gemma commented tartly.

For a split second angry pain gripped Betsy and she pushed restive fingers through the feathery fringe of dark red hair on her pale brow. She almost blurted out that she had had a bloke of her own until Gemma had stolen him and she only bit back that crack with difficulty. The cost of restraint made hot pink flare over her cheekbones and she let her pride do her talking for her and she lied. 'There's a guy at work…I'm seeing him.'

In open disconcertion, her younger sister stared at her. 'What's his name?'

'Joe…' Betsy compressed her lips and looked down at her meal without appetite. The same instant as the untruth had left her lips she'd regretted it, for she realised that that one lie would only lead to further lies. But Joe did exist, she reminded herself, and, while she might not be actually dating him, he had at least asked her out. 'He's new…he started at Imperial two weeks ago—'

'What age is he? What does he look like?' Interested questions flooded from Gemma.

'Late twenties. Tall, broad, fair.' Betsy shrugged, thinking that if she did go out with Joe even once it would magically transform her lie into the truth.

Gemma grinned. 'Well, it's about time—'

Rory was frowning. 'How much do you know about this guy? There are a lot of creeps out there. Be careful,' he urged Betsy.

Gemma's grin fell off her pretty face as though she had been slapped and Betsy could have groaned out loud. Gemma took offence if Rory showed the slightest interest in or concern for her sister. Bowing her head, Betsy got through the awkward silence that followed that comment by scooping up the pyjama-clad toddler who had crept into the room while the adults were talking. Snatched up into a cuddle by her fond aunt, the little girl giggled and turned up an entrancing face. An adorable mix of her parents' genes, Sophie had Rory's dark brown hair matched with Gemma's big blue eyes. Soon after the diversion supplied by her niece's entrance, Betsy announced that she 'really *had* to fly' because she had an early start in the morning.

She had only just got back to her cramped bedsit in Hounslow when her mother phoned her.

'Gemma's really upset…' Corinne Mitchell began, and although a sense of absolute frustration engulfed Betsy at those familiar words she still sat down to dutifully listen.

'I shouldn't have gone over for dinner.' Betsy sighed. 'It just causes friction.'

'There wouldn't be a problem if Rory would just *marry* your poor sister,' her mother lamented. 'There she is, the mother of a two-year-old, and there's still no sign of a wedding ring! Of course she's unhappy. They've got their nice apartment and Rory is doing well as a lawyer. What's he waiting for?'

Betsy drew in a slow, deep sustaining breathe. 'This isn't any of my business, Mum—'

'But you know Rory Bartram better than anyone!' Corinne protested vehemently. 'He's breaking Gemma's heart—'

'Lots of couples live together these days,' Betsy interposed gently.

'Rory wasn't planning to make you live in sin, though, was he?' Corinne snapped out that reminder with audible resentment on her younger daughter's behalf. 'Is it any wonder that Gemma feels terribly hurt when she sees the father of her child paying attention to you?'

'He *wasn't* paying attention to me,' Betsy stressed wearily, but she knew that the older woman was barely listening. All worked up by the spur of a doubtless emotional phone tirade from her younger daughter, Corinne Mitchell was set on having her say about the deficiencies of Gemma's relationship with Rory.

It was a familiar pattern and it hurt Betsy a lot that her mother should be so indifferent to her feelings. Why did she have to be upbraided with the tale of Gemma's problems with Rory? Why was she expected to endure her sister's shrewish comments in forgiving silence? Even less welcome was the wounding bitter note in her mother's voice that implied that it was somehow Betsy's fault that Gemma's world was not as rosy and perfect as she thought it should be.

More and more Betsy was learning that when Gemma was annoyed with her she would be shunned by the rest of her family as well. It would be quite a few weeks before she heard from her mother again. Gemma was very like her mother in looks and personality and Corinne identified closely with Gemma's interests. When she was a kid, Betsy had never questioned the reality that her sister two years her junior was the favoured child. As a baby, Gemma had had a heart murmur and everybody had fussed over her. By the time she'd received a clean bill of health, her parents had been so used to giving her the lion's share of their attention that nothing had changed. Betsy's parents simply idolised Gemma and Sophie was the jewel in her sister's crown.

In comparison, Betsy had always been a bit of a misfit in the Mitchell family circle. Her preferences in clothes and her interests had never been feminine enough to meet with her mother's approval. In fact her happiest childhood memories revolved round her late grandfather, who had restored classic cars in his spare time. As a teenager, she had been a sporty tomboy, obsessed with cars when other girls her age had been obsessed with the boys who drove them. On that front she had been a shy late developer and intimidated by the success of her kid sister in the same department. Boys had started chasing Gemma when she was only thirteen.

Betsy had met Rory at a sports club when she was eighteen. He had been a friend first, but she had known how she'd felt about him long before he'd got around to asking her out. At that point, Betsy killed her forbidden thoughts stone dead. That was the past, she reminded herself sharply. Nobody needed to tell her that no man could be 'stolen' by another woman against his will. Nor, she reflected, should she even have been surprised when Rory had fallen for Gemma, who was much livelier and sexier. That mental slap administered, Betsy got into bed.

The next morning when she arrived at work, Joe

Tyler was already putting a gleaming polish to the bonnet of the car he drove. He was a hard worker, she acknowledged grudgingly, and she questioned her own almost instinctive recoil from him. So he struck her as being a little arrogant and conceited, but he was young, attractive and single and she had met men smug about a great deal less. It was only two weeks since he had joined the staff at Imperial Limousines and he didn't join in with the usual grousing about the awkward hours, the low pay and the demanding and unappreciative customers. In fact, rather like herself, Joe was a loner and a man of few words. How long had it been since she had dated someone? *Too* long, she decided, strolling rather self-consciously closer to the blond man.

'You said you would get tickets for the racing at Silverstone…is the offer still open?'

Joe kept on polishing. 'Maybe…'

Her ready temper sparked her into embarrassed defensiveness. 'Well, when you've made your mind up, tell me. But then maybe *I'll* need—'

'No, you took me up wrong,' Joe protested, planting a large hand on her arm to prevent her walking away again. 'Offer's still open.'

He was built like a rock face and the unease that he had awakened in her before almost surfaced again. Mastering the urge to go into retreat, she managed to smile instead and told herself not to take offence at the smug satisfaction he could barely hide. If Joe Tyler thought she would be a pushover for his muscular charm, he would soon find out how wrong he was…

Six weeks after his previous visit, Cristos flew into London from the South of France.

Timon met him off his flight and handed him a sealed envelope.

Cristos raised a questioning brow. 'What's this?'

'Spyros Zolottas asked me to give it to you before you left the airport.'

Cristos pulled out a brash greetings card signed by his cousin. 'But it's not my birthday,' he said in bewilderment.

Timon looked tense and said nothing. Some minutes later, Cristos came to a halt twenty feet away from the limousine that his PA had indicated across the car park. His mystification came to a sudden end and was replaced by a raw leap of anticipation. He had a photographic memory. It was the same car that had been driven by the beautiful redhead he had admired while in his cousin's company more than a month earlier. He could not initially credit that Spyros could have come up with such a classy surprise.

Timon broke into an urgent explanation, 'Your cousin was determined to surprise you. He said that he would take responsibility for hiring this particular limo company for the weekend but I didn't feel—'

'No need to hyperventilate,' His employer advised in a husky undertone, his bold dark eyes glittering over the female figure already emerging from the driver's seat.

Not even the chauffeur's uniform could conceal her essential perfection. Slender as a reed with a waist that could not be larger than the span of his two hands, she moved with the liquid grace of a dancer. He pictured her in silk. Silk that would slide across her fine skin and feel smooth as satin beneath his hands. It did not cross his mind for even a moment that he might not be able to have her. Whenever he wanted a woman, she came to him. Whichever woman he wanted, he got. Once or twice the strength of his own magnetic pull with her sex had been a curse when the wives and partners of his friends had given him willing and eager signals. But he had never met with failure.

'I should warn you that your security team are very concerned by this last-minute change in your travel arrangements,' Timon continued anxiously. 'There has not even been time to check out this new company.'

'I am entirely content,' Cristos drawled, his whole attention on the young woman pacing round the limo in a last-minute inspection. He sensed her innate pride in the angle of her small head, the straightness of her spine and the upward tilt of her delicate jaw line. Would she be a challenge? He loved a challenge but he was practical too: he only had a weekend to spare.

'It is a much smaller firm…standards of service may not be what you are accustomed to—'

The beginnings of a wicked smile tugged at Cristos' wide, sensual mouth. 'On the other hand, standards of service might be beyond any I have previously received.'

At that point, Timon took the hint and surrendered to the inevitable.

'I'm afraid you'll have to find your own way back to the office today,' Cristos added without hesitation.

An involuntary grin chased the earnest aspect from the younger man's face.

Betsy was in a very prickly mood. Her boss had warned her that the new client was a mega-rich foreign VIP to be treated like a god in the hope of attracting further business. While amazed that an employer who gave all the best opportunities to the men on his staff had selected her as driver, she had been pleased as well. However, before she'd even left for the airport Imperial Limousines had received a visit from Cristos Stephanides' bodyguards. That had caused a stir. Their usual clients were not in the league that required hefty personal security. The bodyguards had not been impressed by the shabby premises that housed the limo firm. They had turned up their noses at the vehicle she was to use, queried her excellent driving credentials and warned her that they would be in close supervision at all times. A bunch of unredeemable sexist pigs, she thought bitterly, who had been busily engaged in patrolling the car park like the cast of a gangster movie ever since her arrival.

Sixth sense warned her that she was under scrutiny. Spinning round, she jerked still at the sight of the male striding towards her. It was as if someone somewhere turned the pace of time to slow motion. He was tall, lean and…and so beautiful that her chest went all tight and she couldn't breathe and couldn't stop looking. But then her brain stepped into the breach and forced her to grab a hold of herself and break free of her own shocking paralysis.

'Mr Stephanides…' Mercifully her voice emerged a little breathless round the edges but calm and quiet in tone.

'And you are…?'

'Betsy Mitchell,' she framed, holding open the door to the rear passenger seat.

'Betsy…' He said her name as if he were savouring something edible and he had a voice like no other she had ever heard before. His drawl had a dark, deep, masculine pitch, a sizzlingly sexy accented edge that sent a quiver down her taut spine. 'So that's what I call you.'

'Mitchell will do, sir,' she answered without expression, throwing up the barrier of their differing status with a strong sense of relief.

Unaccustomed to being contradicted, Cristos glanced down at her. She was not as tall as he had assumed she was from a distance: she was around five feet eight or nine. What was more, her façade of cool professionalism was a fake. He was a trained observer and he could see the almost undetectable tiny nervous tremors assailing her slight length.

'I prefer Betsy,' he murmured softly to make her look up at him.

Disconcerted, she tipped back her head to lift her gaze and met his brilliant dark eyes for the first time. Her mouth ran dry and her heartbeat took off at a sprint. His provocative appraisal dropped to linger on her soft full lips and then roamed on down to the pouting thrust of her breasts before flicking back up again to spell out a message of sexual interest as blatant as a speech.

Deeply shaken, she tore her gaze from his fiercely handsome features. He swung into the car and she closed the door on him. Her palms were damp on the steering wheel. How dared he look her over as if she were on offer to him? Perhaps he had noticed the way she looked at him, a snide little inner voice mocked and a wash of hot, guilty pink warmed her cheeks. What had come over her? He was the fanciable equivalent of a flying saucer. Of course she had stared. Any woman would have stared. Why was she beating herself up about a perfectly natural reaction? The guy was drop dead gorgeous. He was lucky she hadn't stuck a pin in him to check he was real and not an illusion.

Nervous laughter bubbling in her throat, she hit the communication button.

'Everything in order, sir?' she asked.

'There's no still water in the fridge,' he informed her.

And there she had been thinking he would be dazzled by the array of soft drinks available to him! He was supposed to be very rich, she reminded herself, and the rich were reputed to be picky about little details. There was the proof. His refined taste buds could not tolerate sparkling in place of still water. She pulled off the road at the first garage and was in the act of climbing out when he buzzed down the glass partition dividing them. 'Why have we stopped?' he demanded.

Betsy spun back in surprise and leant back into the limo to address him. 'You wanted still mineral water. My boss said your every wish should be my command…'

'I *wish*…' Cristos Stephanides murmured, smooth and soft as velvet.

Staring at him, she was entrapped by his sheer animal magnetism and exotic dark good looks. His luxuriant hair looked very dark against the pale backdrop of the leather head restraint. His bronzed skin was stretched taut over hard masculine cheekbones, an arrogant nose and a beautifully chiselled wide, sensual mouth. With an immense effort, she broke free of the scorching dark golden eyes that were making her tummy flip like a schoolgirl's.

She hurried into the garage shop. Her legs felt like cotton-wool supports. She was in a daze. So he was flirting a little—so what was new? Some guys thought you expected it. Some guys flirted with every woman they met. *I wish* he had said. Why was she suddenly acting and thinking like a ditzy teenager? He made her feel like one. She blinked in bemusement as she turned away from the checkout.

His senior bodyguard, a giant with shoulders the size of tree trunks, barred her passage. 'Who gave you permission to stop the limo without warning us?' he asked in an angry hiss. 'You have left Mr Stephanides in an unlocked vehicle without protection. How could you be so foolish?'

Betsy was astonished by the force of that verbal attack. 'Nobody told me I needed permission or that I should warn you—'

'How else can we do our job? Don't deviate from the agreed route again,' he admonished.

Pale with angry discomfiture, Betsy got back into the car. She passed the mineral water into the rear seat without turning her head and ignited the engine when she heard her passenger speak. She was annoyed at a telling off that she considered unjust. She drove people to functions like weddings and balls and had only once dealt with a minor celebrity. Imperial Limousines was a small firm that did not have a VIP client list. She was not accustomed to dealing with wealthy international businessmen and had not been trained to handle complex security requirements. The sooner she delivered him to his fancy country estate, the happier she would be.

'What happened back there?' Cristos enquired.

'I beg your pardon?' Betsy questioned in turn, face and voice deadpan.

'One of my bodyguards approached you…' Dolius, the head of his security team, whose abrasive personality would never fit him for a diplomatic career. Cristos had watched her green eyes flare with anger while her chin had tilted at a very feminine wounded but stubborn angle. He had been startled by his own urge to leap out of the car and tell Dolius to pick on someone his own size and sex if he wanted a fight.

'Oh, *that*…yes, he was just wondering why I'd pulled off the road,' she advanced with studied lightness.

Dolius had come down on her like a ton of bricks for that impulse, Cristos translated. 'He upset you.'

'No, of course he didn't!' No way was Betsy about to tell tales on another employee whom she had to deal with.

Cristos was furious that she was lying to him. That she was upset was painfully obvious. She was no good at hiding her feelings. She was also driving very, very slowly and making all kinds of restless, unnecessary adjustments to various switches and dials. He was even less pleased when she closed the partition.

Betsy was trying not to think about what a truly horrible week she had had. She had ignored her ESP when it came to Joe Tyler and she had paid the price. A cold shiver of remembrance ran through her. At the end of the first date he had parked the car down an entry and tried to treat her like some hooker he had picked up off the street. She had had to fight him off and he had been very abusive. It had been a seriously scary experience. In the light of that ordeal, she could only marvel at her own adolescent response to Cristos Stephanides. As she hadn't been remotely attracted to Joe, she should never have encouraged him. Cristos Stephanides? He was as safe a fantasy as a poster on a bedroom wall, she decided, and she accelerated down the motorway.

Cristos had never been so comprehensively ignored

by a woman. Having no intention of opening a conversation with the back of her head, he opted for the direct approach. He lifted the car phone to communicate with her. 'Take the next turn off. There's a hotel. We'll stop there for a break.'

'Is this a scheduled stop?' Betsy enquired.

'I don't have a schedule this weekend. I'm not working,' Cristos spelt out.

Betsy tried not to smile at the thought of the mayhem that had to be breaking out in the bodyguards' car when the limo was seen to deviate yet again from the agreed route. But she resisted any urge to glance into the back seat and catch another glimpse of her passenger. At twenty-five years of age, she was too old to be daydreaming like a schoolgirl over a guy she knew nothing about.

Her footsteps crunching over the gravel outside the gracious country hotel, she pulled open the passenger door.

'I hate being locked in a car for hours on end,' Cristos imparted in his rich, dark drawl. 'We'll have coffee.'

She forgot her embargo on looking at him and tipped her head back to encounter brilliant dark golden eyes fringed by black spiky lashes. 'Thank you, sir…but I'll stay with the limo.'

His gaze narrowed. 'That wasn't a request…it was an order.'

Off-balanced by that unhesitating contradiction, she stared at him for a split second too long and then hurriedly dropped her head, her colour fluctuating. Maybe he was keen to ensure that his driver remained alert by taking an adequate break. Fair enough. She locked the car and followed in his arrogant wake. His head bodyguard strode towards them. Cristos Stephanides addressed him in what she assumed to be his own language. Just a handful of brief, softly spoken words and the security man turned pale and backed off with what might have been a hasty apology.

Indoors, engulfed in the ticking-clock silence of the kind of luxury establishment set up to create the atmosphere of a private country house, she was hugely uncomfortable. But it made no impression whatsoever on her companion. He addressed the receptionist with the calm expectancy of a male who had been waited on hand and foot from the day of his birth.

'Sit with me…' With a lean brown hand he indicated an armchair beside the magnificent marble fireplace.

Betsy stared fixedly into the burning embers of the welcoming fire. 'It wouldn't be appropriate, sir.'

'Allow me to decide what's appropriate.'

'But not what I do with my free time. If this is an official break,' Betsy responded with flat clarity, 'I'm entitled to choose how I spend it.'

'Obviously the whip and chair approach is unwise with a woman of your strength of character,' Cristos Stephanides conceded lazily. 'I ask you in all humility…please join me for coffee.'

Involuntary amusement tugged at Betsy. *In all humility?* Was he serious? She almost laughed out loud. He had the extreme poise and arrogant assurance of a male who had never known what humility was. Why was he even making the invitation? What was in it for him?

'Why?' she asked baldly, tipping her head back, eyes as bright as emerald chips gleaming with suspicion.

Theos mou, why was she fighting him? Back at the car park in that very first visual exchange, Cristos had recognised her desire. She had not been able to hide the feverish longing that he had seen on so many female faces since he'd been a teenager. But he could not recall when he had last had to make so much effort. She was not encouraging him. She was making everything difficult. He had got lazy, he acknowledged. His women always did most of the running, but now he was dealing with a female who looked as if she would bolt at the first ill-chosen word or move.

'I feel like company,' he murmured with deliberate casualness, hitching back his powerful personality and swallowing the smarter comments hovering on the tip of his tongue.

Betsy was bemused. A client had never tried to cross the boundaries with her before. She saw no reason why he should be any different. Her uniform was old-fashioned and unflattering. In the course of her working day few men had given her a second glance.

'Are you married?' Cristos asked abruptly, belatedly wondering if there was a reason for her surprising hesitance. 'Living with someone?'

'No…but—'

Cristos curved a confident hand to her spine and urged her down onto the richly upholstered sofa. 'Then join me.'

Unyielding as a stone pillar, she sank down. He took her taut silence in his stride and filled it with the story of a society wedding he had recently attended at the hotel. He was very amusing. She sat there enthralled, unable to take her eyes from his lean, devastating features. Indeed the excuse to watch him was a conscious pleasure and a release from the deprivation of not being able to look. Everything about him fascinated her.

She drank her coffee without tasting it. At his request she took her cap off and coloured at the intensity of his scrutiny. She answered his few questions. She was twenty-five, single, had worked at Imperial for three years, had always wanted to work with cars. That he was not that interested in her answers was not something she judged him on for she initially assumed he was merely making polite conversation. Slowly, very slowly, for she had always held a very modest opinion of her own looks, she realised that Cristos Stephanides actually appeared to be attracted to her and was seeking a response.

At the point where she could no longer mistake his motives and without any hesitation whatsoever, Betsy lifted her cap, replaced it on her head and rose to her feet. 'I'm your driver,' she said bluntly. 'I'm not interested in anything else.'

In fierce disconcertion at that sudden bold assurance, Cristos sprang upright, brilliant dark eyes cool as black ice. 'That's a lie.'

Mortified colour stained her fair skin at that direct contradiction but Betsy still lifted her chin. 'I can admire a painting without wanting to buy it—'

'This situation may be unconventional—'

'There isn't a situation and if there were, it would be tacky.' Betsy was infuriated by his attempt to excuse his behaviour. 'This isn't a social occasion and I wouldn't risk my job for you. I drive limos for a living and you do whatever you do to afford to hire people like me…and that's it—'

'I'm not a snob—'

'No?' A delicate auburn brow rose, questioning that

assertion, green eyes scornful and furious. 'But then you don't need to be. You weren't asking me out on a date, were you? The only invite I was going to get was a sleazy sexual one. Well, no, thank you!'

Cristos wanted to rip the cap off her again and…? His lean brown hands coiled into savage fists. And then do all the sleazy sexual stuff until she was on her knees with gratitude that he had honoured her with his interest. Her attack on him was out of all proportion to anything he had said or done and he was outraged that she had chosen to spring such a scene on him in a public place where he could not freely respond. Across the room, Dolius and his second-in-command were studiously avoiding looking anywhere near him, which told Cristos that they had not missed a single second of the drama. Seething with injured pride and a fierce sense of injustice, Cristos Stephanides watched Betsy Mitchell stalk out of the hotel.

What a smooth, calculating, utterly ruthless bastard, Betsy thought tempestuously, slamming her way into the driver's seat of the limo and still shaking with fury. Had he really believed that he could sweet-talk her into going upstairs to a hotel room with him? For when he'd insisted she join him for coffee that had surely been his intent! Did she look stupid enough to make a mistake of that magnitude? Or so cheap and easy he had assumed she would be a pushover? Had he planned to reward her with an extra large tip? Or his magnificent body? When she saw him approaching in the wing mirror, she sat tight.

Hard jaw line at a stubborn angle, Cristos refused to open the door for himself. He stood there challenging her and, had it been necessary, he would have continued to stand there through thunder, lightning and a force-ten gale to make his point. Clumsy with resentful haste, Betsy finally scrambled out and wrenched open the passenger door for him.

'Thank you,' Cristos breathed, smooth as glass.

She did not believe that she had ever hated another human being so much as she did him at that instant. She drove for an hour with a fierce concentration that shut out every thought. The limo left the motorway for quiet country roads and speed was no longer possible. With scant warning a tractor pulled out of a lane. As the slow vehicle forced a passage out in front of the bodyguards' car Betsy almost smiled at the thought of the annoyance it would cause.

The partition between driver and passenger buzzed down. 'For the record,' Cristos Stephanides breathed with sardonic bite, 'I'm not into sleazy sex.'

'If you want an argument, come back and see me when I'm no longer working for you and forced to be polite,' Betsy snapped.

'Back at the hotel…that was you being *polite*?' Cristos stressed in a derisive tone of wonderment that made her want to stop the limo, leap into the back seat and beat him up.

'You were out of line,' Betsy snapped at him furiously. 'What sort of a guy tries to pull his chauffeur?'

'One who has just become a convert to total snobbery,' Cristos spelt out with maddening assurance.

It was at that point that Betsy saw a male figure crouched down by the side of the road just ahead. That was the only warning she had before something that gleamed metallic and grey in the sunlight was thrown at the car. The wheels ran over it. A tyre blew out and then another, sending the powerful vehicle out of her control into a dangerous swerve. The limo hit the ditch with a thunderous jolt that rattled every bone in her body. Almost simultaneously the door beside her was yanked noisily open.

In disbelief, Betsy saw Joe Tyler peering in at her and momentarily wondered if she was coming round after having been knocked out, for she could not understand how otherwise he could have been there on the spot. 'Joe…?' she framed uncertainly, still reeling from the impact of the crash.

'Have a nice sleep, Betsy.'

Too late she noticed that he had what looked like a gun clutched in his hand. She did not even have time to panic. A tingling pain hit her midriff and she gasped because without warning her limbs seemed to turn to jelly. Joe thrust her aside with no more care than he would have accorded a sack. Just before she passed out she heard him speak again, but what he said made little sense to her.

'Imagine a bloke like you fancying my girl-friend…well, you both deserve a surprise!'

The black claustrophobic cloud of oblivion rolled in over Betsy and her body slumped down on the seat. Within seconds her passenger was in the same condition.

CHAPTER TWO

CRISTOS recovered consciousness first.

Instantly he came alert and defied any awareness of physical discomfort to spring off the bed on which he had been lying. His keen dark eyes took on a dazed aspect as he struggled to get a handle on his unfamiliar surroundings. He studied the unconscious woman still on the bed with scorching intensity. The ubiquitous cap had gone and straying strands of bright Titian hair feathered her brow. Her skin was white as snow. Like Mary's little lamb in the nursery rhyme? A harsh laugh escaped Cristos but there was nothing of humour in it.

What a very dangerous distraction Betsy Mitchell had proved to be! There was nothing more galling to Cristos than the awareness that he had allowed a woman to lead him into a prearranged trap. It was poetic justice however that she had been double crossed by her partners in crime and abandoned to the tender mercies of their victim. No doubt she would learn the hard way that Cristos would choose death over victimhood any day.

Fierce thirst brought Betsy out of her stupor. Even before she opened her eyes, she knew she felt dreadful. Her limbs felt as heavy as leaden weights. She was also incredibly hot and it was that awareness that first roused her to register that something was wrong. She was wearing clothes and she never lay down fully dressed. In the same moment as she lifted her lashes on an unfamiliar room, she remembered Joe attacking

29

her. She pressed a hand to her midriff, felt a slight soreness there and tore off her uniform jacket to lift her shirt and touch the tiny red puncture wound. A sense of complete unbelief enveloped her. He must have shot her with some sort of tranquilliser dart because she had passed out. But why would Joe have done such a thing? *Cristos!* Cristos Stephanides. Where on earth was he?

In the grip of fear and horror that Joe was some kind of maniac who had kidnapped her because she had rejected him, Betsy scrambled upright. She was only wearing one shoe and there was no sign of the missing one. Kicking off the one that remained, she raced out of the bedroom and headed straight for the wide open door several feet beyond.

In that doorway, Betsy came to a breathless halt. She blinked. Her lower lip parted company from the upper in an inelegant expression of astonishment. Barely a hundred feet away a shimmering sea as crystal-blue as the sky above was washing a sandy beach. The beauty of the scene struck her as incongruous and she thought she had to be hallucinating. When she had lost control of the limo, it had been raining. It had been a typical English spring day: sunny and damp in turns with a breeze thrown in for good measure. But the heat of the golden sun above seemed Mediterranean.

Cristos strode into view from behind the rocks girding the northern edge of the beach. Her tummy flipped. Intense relief filled her. He was safe and, whether it was logical or not, his presence made her feel less afraid. As he drew closer she charted the changes in his once immaculate appearance. He had doffed his suit jacket and tie. A pearl-grey shirt open at his brown throat outlined his broad shoulders. His black hair was tousled and a heavy growth of dark stubble outlined his stubborn jaw line and wide, sensual mouth. He still looked spectacular. Her tummy performed another somersault. His hardcore sexuality had a powerful charge.

Seeing her, Cristos came to a halt. Glittering dark eyes zeroed in on her, his lean, handsome features clenching into formidable stillness. 'Where are we?' he asked roughly.

Her brow furrowed, for she could not understand why he should ask her that question in a tone that implied that she would have that information at her fingertips. 'I don't know...do you?'

'How the hell would I know? Don't play dumb with me,' Cristos warned her.

Her spine stiff with tension and forgetting that she was not wearing shoes, Betsy moved out onto the sun-warmed path. The surface was uncomfortably hot for soles encased only in nylon tights and she hurried into the sparse shade thrown by the gnarled tree that grew at the front of the house. 'Play dumb? I don't understand—'

'I know that you were involved in plotting my kidnapping—'

'You know...*what*?'

'You must've been shattered to wake up here and realise that your fellow conspirators had decided to ditch you—'

'My fellow conspirators? What on earth are you accusing me of?' Betsy fired back at him in frank bewilderment.

'You greeted the gorilla who shot us both full of knock-out drugs by name.'

Her brain, she discovered in frustration, was very reluctant to process thoughts with anything like its usual efficiency. Gorilla? Did he mean Joe? Of course Joe was involved in the kidnapping because he had attacked them both. 'Joe works for Imperial Limousines…I didn't appreciate what was happening when he first opened the car door—'

'You said his name quite happily,' Cristos Stephanides countered.

'I was in shock…I hadn't had enough time to appreciate that the crash hadn't been an accident.' She lifted an unsteady hand to her brow, which was damp as much with stress as with the unfamiliar heat. She pulled out the clip anchoring her hair and let it fall, massaging the back of her neck where the clip had left a tender spot. 'That was a stinger that was hurled in front of the car to puncture the tyres and force us to a stop, wasn't it?'

Cristos surveyed her with brooding intensity. 'If you're trying to convince me that you're innocent of any involvement, you're wasting your breath. You are also making me angry—'

Her anxiety growing, Betsy gazed back at him. 'You're serious, aren't you? But you can't decide that I'm a criminal just because I know Joe—'

'I don't think I'm quite that simplistic.' Cristos dealt her a derisive look.

'How could I not know him when he works in the same place?'

'Oh, I think the connection between you and Joe was a touch more intimate than that,' Cristos murmured with scathing softness.

Betsy was exceedingly reluctant to accept that he

might be implying a certain fact that she was in no hurry to tell him. 'What do you mean?'

'He referred to you as his girlfriend.'

The guilty colour ran up hot beneath her skin. Too late she recalled Joe making some crack in that line before she'd lost consciousness. 'I went out with him once…OK?'

'No, it's not OK. Nothing about this situation is OK.' His lean, hard-boned face was grim. 'You're involved in this filthy business right up to your throat—'

'Look, if you dated a serial killer once, would you be responsible for her crimes?' Betsy threw at him. He was being so unfair to her. She was ashamed and embarrassed that she had ever gone out with someone of Joe's evident propensities. But surely nothing she had said or done could possibly have contributed to the current situation?

'I haven't got time for this nonsense…' Cristos strode forward and closed lean hands to her forearms. 'I've been kidnapped. My life is at risk. I have no plans to sit around on a deserted island in the middle of an ocean waiting for the kidnappers' next move—'

'We're on an island?' Betsy interrupted in dismay, wincing a little at the strength of those long, tensile fingers, which were biting just a tad uncomfortably into her arms.

She had always considered herself to be a fair height. However, Cristos Stephanides had to be around six feet four inches tall. He towered over her to such an extent that she felt tiny. Indeed she was beginning to feel actively intimidated by him. He was very strong and he was very angry and he was not listening to her. Could she blame him for that? He *had* been kidnapped. His life probably was at risk. Whether she liked it or not she could understand why he should be highly suspicious of a woman who appeared to have been on terms of familiarity with one of his kidnappers.

'Where is this island?' Cristos demanded harshly. 'I need to know everything that you know so that I can work out what's coming next!'

'But I don't *know* anything…' In a sudden movement that took him by surprise, Betsy tore herself free and backed hurriedly away from him. 'You've got to believe me about that—'

Unafraid to turn up the pressure, Cristos advanced. 'I don't. You were the bait, and very effective bait. I went for it—'

Her slender length rigid, Betsy slowly increased the distance between them with quiet, cautious steps. Her nervous antenna was on a high state of alert. After all, what did she know about Cristos Stephanides and how violent he might be in such circumstances? He believed she had conspired with his kidnappers and might feel that his need for information was justification for getting rough. She found it bitterly ironic that just ten days earlier she would have stood her ground against Cristos, blithely confident that she could look after herself and that most men were essentially decent. It was Joe Tyler who had taught her to fear masculine strength. He had held her against her will long enough to teach her to be scared and had for ever stolen her peace of mind in male company.

'I wasn't the bait,' Betsy swore, fighting to put as much weight and sincerity into her voice as she could while at the same time wondering what the heck he was talking about. 'I had nothing to do with your kidnapping and I was as shocked by all this as you are.'

'Like hell you were,' Cristos growled, watching the sunlight pick up the deep coppery tints in the fantastic rippling coil of hair sliding across her shoulders with her every movement. He was convinced she had let her hair down in an effort to distract him. 'You were a part of it right up until your boyfriend decided to sacrifice you—'

'He isn't my boyfriend…he's a creep I went out with one time!' Betsy launched back at him in frustration.

'I won't accept your lies. I want answers from you and I want them fast.' Lean, strong face hard with determination, Cristos surveyed her with merciless dark eyes. 'You have put my life at risk and you owe me, so start talking…'

The menacing chill he exuded scared her. She felt that an unspoken threat hung in the air between them. The very tone of his dark, deep drawl sent a shiver licking down her taut spinal cord. In a sudden movement, she spun on her heel and took off across the beach. He shouted after her, called her name but she just ran even faster.

Cristos swore long and low. He had seen the stark fear blossoming at the back of her eyes and done nothing to assuage it. Was she used to men who lashed out with their fists? That concept shook him. He had never hurt a woman in his life. No woman had ever looked at him in that way before. No woman had ever had cause. He released his breath in a raw exhalation, acknowledging that he had been prepared to use her fear to his own advantage. His continuing health could well depend on what he could learn from Betsy Mitchell, but frightening her had been a wrong move.

Betsy cut up through the sand dunes and scattered

the clutch of small wiry sheep grazing there. 'Relax,' she told them apologetically, but they kept their distance.

Just as she would keep her distance from Cristos Stephanides until his temper had had time to cool, she decided. In spite of the heat she still felt cold when she thought about Joe Tyler. She doubted that that was even his real name, for he had only come to work at Imperial Limousines *after* the Stephanides booking had been made. No wonder Joe hadn't mixed with the other men. His objective must always have been the kidnapping of Cristos Stephanides. But she was mystified as to why Joe Tyler had shown such a keen interest in her from the outset and asked her out.

She sheltered from the sun under a clump of trees and tried not to think about how desperately thirsty she was. She could still see the terracotta roof of the stone house and beyond it another smaller building. A boathouse? A slipway ran between it and the jetty. In every direction she looked the views of sparkling turquoise sea, pale golden sand and lush green vegetation were incredibly beautiful. But she would have given them all up just for a drink. But how were the sheep surviving? Somewhere, she registered, there had to be fresh water.

Trees overhung the stream she found and the water ran so clear that she could see the colour of every pebble. Using her hand as a scoop, she drank deep and long and splashed her face into the bargain. Drowsiness overwhelmed her then and in the cool of the shaded bank she pillowed her head on her arms and let herself sleep.

Betsy wakened with a start, glanced at her watch and realised that she had been dead to the world for hours.

Dusk was beginning to roll in and she scrambled upright and headed back in the direction of the beach.
On the way there she stumbled and cut her foot on a
sharp stone. Peeling off her ruined tights, she exam-
ined the wound. It was bleeding freely and she grimaced and ripped up the tights to make an impromptu
bandage. Someone had once told her that salt water
could act like an antiseptic and she limped with difficulty across the sand and clambered onto the rocks
that stretched out into the sea to find a place where
she could safely bathe her foot.

Cristos was finishing his fifth complete circuit of the
island. As the afternoon had worn on into evening and
he could still find no trace of Betsy Mitchell his concern had grown in proportion. He had searched every
possible hiding place and come up with nothing. When
he saw her standing on the promontory his relief was
immense. He strode across the beach towards her. She
was standing on one slender leg like a heron but she
lacked the bird's one-legged balance and she was
swaying in apparent indifference to danger on the edge
of the rocks washed by the surf.

'Betsy…come back from there!' Cristos launched
at her in the command intonation that always extracted
instant unquestioning obedience from his employees.

Betsy was startled by that formidable intervention
when in the very act of dipping her throbbing foot into
the rock pool she had discovered, and her head flew
up. Her attempt to twist round and see him was her
downfall because she lost her balance. Her toes had
no grip on the slippery rock and she went flying back-
wards into the sea with a shriek of dismay. She pan-
icked, for the water was deep and the current strong.

She was sinking below the surface for the second time, hands frantically beating at the surf, when Cristos, who had never moved so fast in his life, dived in.

She thought her lungs were going to burst. Strong arms grabbed her and buoyed her up out of the water again where she coughed and spluttered and struggled to suck in enough oxygen to satisfy herself. He swam back to the shore with her and heaved her up the beach.

'I'm OK...' she gasped.

He said something raw in Greek but the hands that held her were surprisingly gentle. The terror that had engulfed her in those frightening seconds when she had been in the water alone brought a shocked surge of tears to her eyes and, although she was struggling to hold them back, a stifled sob escaped her.

Recognising the depth of her distress, Cristos helped her back towards the house. 'What have you done to your foot?'

'I cut it...'

Lean, strong face taut, he bent down and scooped her up to carry her indoors. When he set her down in a bathroom, she was shaking. 'You're all right. Nothing is going to happen to you. Nobody is going to harm you,' Cristos asserted fiercely. 'You are safe with me...OK?'

She collided with lustrous dark golden eyes and her heartbeat limbered up as if she were about to go for a sprint. 'OK...'

'Let me look at your foot.' He sat her down on the cushioned wicker chair and turned up her sole, ebony brows drawing together when he saw the gash.

'I want a bath,' she whispered.

'You should stay out of the water with that cut.'

'I smell like seaweed...' Betsy pointed out.

'And look like a mermaid...' Cristos stared down at her. Drenched, her hair was more vibrant than ever but the sun had flushed her pale skin and her clear eyes were as bright and changeable a blue-green as the sea he loved.

'Something fishy about my legs?' she teased.

He looked. He knew he shouldn't because his body was already reacting to the mere presence of hers with a ferocious craving that not even his usual rock-solid discipline could kill. 'You have incredible legs,' he told her truthfully, for those slim thighs, elegant knees, narrow ankles and amazingly tiny feet of hers were in his far-from-humble opinion amazing works of art.

She went pink and, suddenly shy of him, she got up to run herself a bath. 'I'll be quick,' she muttered, belatedly recognising the reality that his clothes were wet as well.

He glanced back from the door, inky black lashes low over his brilliant incisive eyes. 'You can't swim. Don't go dancing on the rocks again,' he warned her drily.

'I wasn't dancing...I was trying to bathe that cut in salt water to prevent infection—'

'You were willing to risk blood-poisoning and drowning sooner than return here?' Cristos dealt her a stark look of impatience. 'Stop dramatising yourself—'

Betsy went brick-red with embarrassment. 'I don't dramatise myself—'

'What else were you doing when you ran away from me?' Cristos slung back with scorn. 'I don't abuse women. Have you got that straight, because I don't want to waste any more time chasing after you? I spent all afternoon searching high and low for you when I should have been concentrating on more important issues—'

'I didn't ask you to go looking for me. For goodness' sake, I was upset. I wake up feeling like hell and find myself in a totally strange place with a very angry guy…' Recalling the fact that that same guy had undoubtedly saved her life when he'd rescued her from the sea, she squirmed at the awareness that she had yet to thank him for that feat. 'Thanks for getting me out of the water,' she added in a small voice.

'No problem. I wouldn't dream of letting harm come to you,' Cristos contended silkily. 'If you *were* part of the kidnapping plot, I want you all in one piece to hand over to the police.'

Betsy sent him a furious look from eyes that flashed like emeralds. 'Get out of here!'

Wide shoulders thrown back, long, lean, powerful length fluid, Cristos sauntered out. On the other side of the door he smiled. It was very easy to get a rise out of her.

Betsy slid into the sunken bath that was embellished with water jets and set in a surround of exquisite multicoloured mosaic tiles. The floor was made of marble. No expense had been spared. The house might look delightfully rustic on the outside but from what little she had noted indoors the finish was more in the luxury millionaire class. Were kidnappers usually so generous to their victims?

Her hair rinsed and squeaky clean, Betsy wrapped herself in a big fleecy towel and padded back out to the bedroom. It rejoiced in Mediterranean-blue painted walls, a giant bed with a carved wood headboard and crisp white lace-edged linen bedding.

Cristos appeared in the doorway. Hair brushed back from his brow and clean-shaven, he was so incredibly attractive that just one look deprived her of the ability to breathe. 'I used the shower outside.'

In some disconcertion she studied his exquisitely tailored beige chinos and his short-sleeved black shirt. 'Where did you get the clean clothes?

'My weekend case travelled with us. Let me have a look at your foot. I found a first-aid kit in the kitchen.'

His hands were cool on her warm skin. His luxuriant black hair gleamed in the fading light arrowing through the window and she was horribly tempted to curve her fingers to his handsome head. Hands curling in on themselves to resist a level of temptation that was new to her, she sat very still while he demonstrated how extremely resourceful he could be with antiseptic and plasters.

'I'll loan you a shirt,' he murmured, vaulting upright again.

Finding that she was too self-conscious to look at him, she turned away, wondering why she got so embarrassed and tongue-tied around him. 'Nothing here is what you expect,' she muttered to fill the silence.

'Isn't it? I think this is an upmarket honeymooners' retreat that has been hired purely for our benefit. In the room next door there's a most incongruous arrangement of flowers and a bottle of celebration champagne awaiting us.'

'A honeymooners' retreat?' She grabbed at the shirt he tossed.

'The perfect place. Someone choosing to vacation on a tiny deserted island doesn't want company so whoever is in charge of this place won't visit. I imagine that there was a radio here for communication in the event of an emergency but that has naturally been removed.'

Betsy slid her arms into the blue shirt and began carefully to roll up the sleeves. Having buttoned the shirt, she gave the towel a discreet jerk to detach it. Watching her, watching her even when he knew he should not, possessed of the very knowledge that she was naked beneath his shirt; Cristos was endeavouring to get a grip on a powerful surge of rampant lust. His own weakness angered him. She was the gorilla's girl-friend. He was damned if he wanted a kidnapper's leavings. The cotton was so fine he could see the pale pink crests of her pert breasts, the faint hint of tantal-ising shadow below her belly. He was damned beyond all hope of reclaim. It was the weird situation, Cristos assured himself grimly. It was making him act out of character, it was making him behave like a testoster-one-charged teenager who had only had sex in his own imagination.

'Right now all I care about is eating.' Betsy stepped past him out into the spacious reception room beyond. 'Please tell me there's food.'

'Do you cook?'

Betsy entered the pristine kitchen. 'Abysmally... strong men have been known to weep at my table,' she lied, heading straight for the fridge.

'How did you comfort them?' Cristos enquired hus-kily.

Hot colour ran in revealing ribbons across her cheeks. 'I was joking.'

Colliding unwarily with scorching golden eyes, she felt dizzy but the invisible buzz in the air was wick-edly exhilarating. Her skin felt prickly, hot, tight. Her breasts felt full, the pointed tips taut and tender. At the heart of her, she *felt*…She burned with shame when she realised that just being around Cristos Stephanides excited her in a physical way. That had never happened to her before, not even with Rory. Tearing her troubled gaze from Cristos, she became a hive of cooking activity to give her thoughts a safer focus.

'How much food is there?' she asked, refusing to look in his direction lest that indecent sexual longing seize hold of her again and he somehow divine how she was reacting to him.

'Plenty…'

He watched while she made a stir-fry with staggering speed and efficiency. He was as impressed as a guy who had never even boiled a kettle for himself could be.

'How do you think they transported us here?' Betsy enquired when she sat down at the table to eat.

'My bet is that we were smuggled out as cargo from a private airfield and then brought the last stage of the journey by boat. An odd way to travel home,' Cristos quipped.

'Home?'

'This is a Greek island.'

'You can't know that for sure.'

Burnished golden eyes sought and challenged hers. 'I know. I am Greek and the very air here smells of my homeland.'

Betsy said nothing and ate her meal. He was the sort of guy who always set her back up. He was so full of himself, so arrogant. He knew everything. He even knew things he couldn't possibly know. Rising from the table, she said stiffly, 'I'm going to bed.'

'You should make the most of your rest,' Cristos murmured equably. 'We'll be up at dawn. We need to gather enough wood to light a bonfire and keep it burning. If the smoke is noticed hopefully someone will come to investigate.'

It was a good idea but she didn't say so because she had decided that he was already well aware of how clever he was. She slid into the cool of the bed, let her weary limbs sink into the comfortable mattress. Somewhere between closing her eyes and stretching out she fell asleep.

A dark male drawl that was already becoming familiar wakened Betsy again. She was deliciously warm and relaxed. 'We should get up...'

Her lashes lifted and she focused with drowsy admiration on the darkly handsome male face above hers. His black lashes were impossibly long and lush, unnecessary enhancements to eyes of lustrous gold. He was breathtakingly good-looking and devastatingly masculine, two traits that even she recognised were rarely found in one package.

'I want you to know this is a first,' Cristos informed her steadily. 'I've never slept with a woman before and not had sex.'

For a split second, Betsy lay there just staring up at him and then the implications of that sardonic assurance of his sank in. Eyes bright with accusation, a feverish flush on her cheeks, she hugged the sheet to her and sat up. 'You *shared* this bed with me last night?'

CHAPTER THREE

CRISTOS watched with a maddening air of scientific interest as Betsy lurched out of the bed in comical haste. It shook him that she looked so good first thing in the morning. Coppery red hair flying in tousled waves round her oval face and sheathed only in his crumpled shirt, she was very sexy.

'You don't need to act as if you've never shared a bed with a man before,' he said very drily.

'I haven't!' Betsy launched back at him. 'Nor is it something I can treat like a joke.'

Cristos had never felt less like laughing. 'Are you saying that you're…gay?'

Betsy froze and then shook her bright head in wonderment. 'You really don't know where I'm coming from, do you?'

Relaxing from his worst-case scenario, Cristos reclined back against the pillows. 'When you said you'd never shared a bed with a guy, you were obviously exaggerating.'

Betsy folded her arms. Furious as she was with him, she was beginning in a funny way to enjoy herself. 'And how do you make that out?'

'I very much doubt that you're telling me you're a virgin.'

'Why?' Betsy heard herself say defensively. 'Did you think I would be ashamed of the fact?'

Silence fell, a silence so thick and heavy it screamed at her. Cristos could not conceal his surprise. Her face

45

burned with colour. Wishing she had kept her mouth firmly closed on the subject, she vanished into the bathroom. Why was she embarrassed by what she had just revealed? She had always been shy and Rory had been her only serious boyfriend. Two months after she had begun dating him, he had gone abroad to work for a year. Against the odds they had stayed together, but when Rory had finally returned to London Betsy had been reluctant to rush into intimacy with him. Even though he had asked her to marry him, she had felt that she needed more time to get to know him again and her caution had strained their relationship. Her sister had stepped into that breach.

A virgin. She was a virgin. Was that what was different about her? Cristos asked himself in bewilderment. His every expectation had been violently overthrown. He wondered why she should suddenly seem more desirable than ever. The strength of his own desire was beginning to exasperate him. She was just a woman like other women. Sexual hunger was simply an appetite to be satisfied. There was nothing special or different about her. But he *was* in dire need of another cold shower. Thrusting back the sheet, he told himself how fortunate he was that that was all that was available.

Betsy was astounded to find women's clothing hanging in one of the bedroom units. 'Whom do you think these belong to?' she asked when she heard Cristos behind her.

Cristos reached over her shoulder and drew out a woman's dress. 'This looks brand-new—'

'Tacky taste…' Betsy held the garment against her slim body, soft mouth down curving at the fact that it was strappy, low-necked and short. She swooped with delight on a pair of mules, hauled them out and dug her feet in. The mules were a good size too large but a great deal preferable to bare feet.

'It all seems to be beach wear…you might as well use it.' Cristos checked the size on an item and reckoned it would fit her like a glove. Coincidence? He didn't think so. Someone had put a great deal of planning into their reception on the island. He was not at all surprised to open the other unit and discover a selection of male apparel.

After checking that her injured foot was already well on the way to healing, Cristos went off to shave. Betsy donned a purple bikini and tied a sparkly blue sarong round her slender waist. The air was still cool before the build-up of the day's heat. The front door was wide and she hovered to drink in the beauty of the fresh dawn light filtering down over the sea and the pale sand while the sun rose in crimson splendour in the east. Finally tearing herself from the view, she noticed the champagne bottle still parked beside the flowers that Cristos had mentioned. Already the petals were dropping from the blooms. As she lifted the vase the sheet of paper that had been tucked between it and the champagne slid down flat on the table surface. Someone had typed several lines of a foreign language in large print on the paper.

'Cristos…' She went pink as she realised how easily his name came to her lips because she thought of him that way. 'What's this?' she asked, extending it to him as he appeared in the bedroom doorway.

An ebony brow lifted as he studied the sheet. 'This is in Greek…where did you get it from?'

'It was on the table…'

His brilliant dark gaze narrowed. 'It wasn't there yesterday.'

'But it must've been,' Betsy pointed out.

'If it had been there I would've seen it,' Cristos breathed with implacable assurance.

'I only saw it when I lifted the vase,' Betsy proffered in consolation. 'For goodness' sake, what does it say?'

Lean jaw line clenching, Cristos vented a harsh laugh. 'It's a load of rubbish. It says that we will not be harmed and that whether the ransom is paid or not, we'll be set free. As if you didn't know!'

Betsy stiffened, her bemusement complete. 'What are you talking about?'

'*This!*' Cristos crushed the notepaper in one powerful fist and let it drop at her feet again in a blatant gesture of contempt. 'It wasn't here yesterday. Therefore you must have planted it.'

'Me…plant it? Are you crazy?' Betsy countered in disbelief.

'If this is an attempt to persuade me to accept my imprisonment here, it's failed,' Cristos spelt out rawly. 'Right now the only person who concerns me is my grandfather, Patras. He's eighty-three and tough as they come. He's already buried my parents and my little sister. But he may not have the strength to survive the stress of my disappearance and the threat of another loss!'

Betsy was very tense. 'Do you think I'm not concerned about my own family? I don't know why you're so suspicious of me—'

'How can I be anything else? You presented me with that stupid note which doesn't make any sense. No more sense than anything else in this scenario,'

Cristos contended in unconcealed frustration. 'I've been kidnapped but, instead of being chained up in a cellar, I'm on a beach in reasonable comfort with a sexy redhead thrown in for good measure.'

'Count your blessings…next time I see a note around here, I'll just pretend not to see it. You haven't given me one good reason why you should still suspect me of having been involved with the kidnappers.'

'There's been too many coincidences,' Cristos delivered, lean, powerful face brooding. 'I saw you for the first time in my life six weeks ago—'

'Six weeks ago…*how*?' Betsy pressed in surprise.

'The wind blew your hat off and you were chasing it in a car park at the airport. You didn't see me. I thought you were gorgeous.' Dark golden eyes that seemed laden with condemnation rested on her.

Betsy had no memory of the occasion but her angry resentment was already starting to ebb away. He had noticed her six weeks back? Actually remembered her? Decided she was 'gorgeous'? She went positively pink with pleasure.

'But it never occurred to me that I'd see you again. I returned to London yesterday and, courtesy of my cousin, you'd been hired to drive me over the weekend.'

'What did your cousin have to do with it?'

'Spyros made the arrangements to bypass the usual limo company and use the one where you work instead. You were supposed to be my surprise.'

Her teeth gritted. No longer did the fact that he had found her instantly attractive seem like a compliment! No longer did she need to wonder why her boss had selected her for the plum job. The cousin would have specifically requested that she be the driver. Indeed the whole scenario that Cristos had depicted outraged her sense of decency.

'Your cousin thought that my services could be hired along with the car, did he?' Betsy fired a look at Cristos from stormy emerald eyes.

Faint colour scored his hard cheekbones. 'That is not what I said. My cousin's intervention simply gave me the chance to meet you. That's all.'

'That's very far from all,' Betsy contradicted, her hands knotting into furious fists as she rejected that much more mild interpretation of the facts. 'Speaking as the woman who was supposed to be your *"surprise"*, I have to admit that I've never heard anything more sexist or disgusting!'

Cristos stayed cool. 'That's your prerogative. I thought you were hot and I welcomed the opportunity to get to know you.'

'You waited less than two hours before you lured me into a hotel and tried to get off with me. Is that why you accused me of being bait? Your seedy cousin goes in search of me, sets me up and I get the blame for it because you have the misfortune to be kidnapped while I'm driving you?' Temper was leaping higher and higher inside Betsy.

'I took risks I would not normally take. I disregarded the advice of my staff. I paid no heed to my own personal security because I was more interested in you—'

'My goodness,' Betsy cut in as citrus-fresh and acidic in tone as a lemon. 'I even get blamed for your overactive libido.'

'Are you always this aggressive to guys who might try to separate you from your virginity?'

Betsy hit him a resounding slap and then fell back a step in shock at what she had done.

'Is that the best you can do?' Cristos asked in silken provocation. 'You'd have done more damage if you'd hit me with your fist—'

'I didn't want to damage you...I'm sorry I slapped you,' Betsy forced out that admission for the sake of form and averted her guilty gaze from the faint mark she had left across the proud angle of a bronzed cheekbone.

'Forgiveness has a price. You let me kiss you.'

Betsy lifted her head, green eyes bright and incredulous.

He shrugged a broad shoulder with immense cool. 'And if you hate it, I'll never do it again.'

Her cheeks warming, Betsy shifted off one foot to the other and back again. 'Of course I would hate it. Save yourself the embarrassment,' she advised him thinly. 'Not five minutes ago you were accusing me of having planted that daft note.'

Glittering dark-as-night eyes met hers and flamed gold. 'But intelligence doesn't come into this. I'm like a drunk who keeps falling off the wagon. I still want to taste you...'

Her breathing fractured in her throat. He was so close she could feel the heat of his male body warming the taut, bare skin of her midriff. A tiny little quiver started deep down inside her, fanning a spark in her pelvis. Her back arched a little. Her mouth ran dry. Slowly, more slowly than her nerves could bear, he lowered his handsome dark head. Common sense told her to back off but longing kept her still on a high of anticipation.

'I'm going to hate this,' she warned him, fighting

to the last ditch, willing herself to find all bodily contact with him revolting.

His wide, sensual mouth came down on hers and, on her terms, it was instant spontaneous combustion. It was like every kiss she had ever dreamt of in her teens and never received. Shell-shocked by the pleasure, she wrapped her arms round him to stay upright. He tasted divine. In fact everything about him might have been specially picked to please her. When he at last lifted his head to drag in some necessary oxygen, she subsided into his lean, powerful frame, losing herself with voluptuous delight in the heady masculine scent of his skin and the awesomely pleasurable feel of him against her. Scanning her feverishly flushed face with smouldering dark golden eyes, he crushed her even closer to him and went back for more of her luscious mouth.

In a fever, Betsy traded kiss for kiss. He employed his tongue with erotic expertise and she gasped, clung to him for support. Again and again she let her own craving rule her, unable to make the break that she knew she should. Her body was all heat and urgency and demand. That fierce hunger she had never felt before was winning the battle between control and restraint.

'Let's go to bed…' Cristos breathed with husky ferocity.

Striving to hide her disconcertion at how fast things had moved, not to mention her overpowering awareness of her own failure to resist him, Betsy looked up. Lean, hard-boned face taut, Cristos gazed down at her. Her knees were ready to buckle. The breathing space had changed nothing. She still wanted him regardless of pride, intelligence or self-respect. A wild, wicked wanting had been born inside her and had created a need so powerful it shocked her.

Cristos let lean brown fingers glide up from her waist to rest against her narrow ribcage. She was extraordinarily conscious of the swollen tenderness of her breasts, the sensation of forbidden warmth between her thighs. In fact she could hardly breathe for excitement and he knew it. In his stunning dark golden gaze burned all the unashamed expectation of a male accustomed to women who met his every demand without hesitation.

Betsy stiffened and fought her own weakness. With an effort, she parted her reddened lips and said hoarsely, 'The bonfire…we were going to build a bonfire…'

Disbelief flaring through him, Cristos watched her walk to the door. That she cannoned into a chair on her passage there was his only consolation.

Outside in the fresh air, Betsy lifted unsteady hands to her hot face and then dropped them hastily again in case he realised just how badly shaken up she was.

'Are you trying to tell me that you hated being touched by me?' Cristos demanded as he joined her, his Greek accent very strong.

She stole a glance at his bold bronzed profile and strove to suppress the inner quiver of response that sought to betray her. 'No but I don't want this to go any further…it's madness,' she told him gruffly.

'You may have a point,' Cristos murmured with a smooth acceptance that disconcerted her. 'I have no contraception here. I assume you're not protected—?'

'No, I'm not,' Betsy slotted in, reddening to the roots of her hair and hurriedly directing her attention elsewhere. He made her feel horribly immature. She was affronted by his assumption that a few kisses could have persuaded her straight into bed with him and his frank reference to the need for contraception embarrassed her. It infuriated her even more that he could switch off and be so cool and rational about the halt that she had called when she herself felt as a weak and stupid as an accident victim fighting shock.

And Betsy was in deep and genuine shock. Shock that she could be so passionate. But most of all shock that a man she barely knew could make her want him infinitely more than she had ever wanted Rory. Rory's kisses had not wiped out her brain cells or made her shiver with lust. She had never been at risk of losing control with Rory. She had honestly believed that she was not a very sexual person but Cristos had just taught her differently.

'The best place to build a fire as a beacon is on the headland at the northern end of the beach,' Cristos pronounced, digging hands balled into fists into the pockets of his tailored chinos in a determined effort to conceal how aroused he still was.

'I think we should scout around before picking a spot,' Betsy heard herself say, reacting to a barely understood urge to always disagree with him.

'Any passing shipping will be able to see a fire there.'

While she listened, Cristos produced another three excellent reasons why his site was the superior, indeed the only possible choice. When he began talking about shelter, wind speed and burn rates she knew herself to be utterly outclassed and subsided into her assigned role of being the willing worker directed by the mastermind.

There was a lot of driftwood scattered on the beach

below the headland and she gathered it piece by piece and carted it uphill to the designated area. Cristos, she learned, left nothing to chance. The fire was laid with geometric exactitude and the wood pile for feeding it was no exception.

'Your shoulders will burn in this heat. Go and put on a top,' Cristos instructed her as the flames smouldered.

'I'm fine,' Betsy framed tartly, temper on a thin leash after a lengthy period of hard physical labour in temperatures she was unaccustomed to working in. 'Why don't you just leave me to look after me?'

'How can I?' Cristos dealt her a glittering golden glance and elevated a derisive ebony brow. His shirt was hanging open to reveal a bronzed torso that rivalled the sculptured perfection of a marble statue. 'You're useless at it!'

Emerald eyes shimmering with rage, Betsy sucked in a great gush of air. 'And on what do you base that staggering assumption?'

'Where do you want me to begin?' Cristos sliced back with relish. 'When you got us kidnapped by not even locking the car door? When you cut your foot? Almost drowned? And you wonder why I should feel that it's my responsibility to ensure that you don't roast yourself alive?'

In a violent movement, Betsy chucked down the log she was dragging. 'You're just furious with me because I won't sleep with you!'

Cristos plunged down the sand bank towards her and scooped her right off her startled feet.

'What are you doing?' she screeched at him.

'I want you to look at yourself in the mirror and then tell me you're not going to cover up—'

'Put me down right now!' Betsy roared at him.

With exaggerated care, Cristos lowered her to the sand. 'I don't like being shouted at,' he warned her, smooth as silk.

'I don't like being lifted like I'm a toy doll! I don't like being ordered round all the time either—'

'Isn't it strange that you should have chosen to become a chauffeur?'

'I'm only filling in time until I start up my own business!' she yelled back at him.

'You'd be wise to get some professional advice before you venture into business on your own behalf,' Cristos pronounced in the most superior of tones.

Fit to be tied, Betsy studied him with outraged green eyes. 'You're a living, breathing miracle, Cristos.'

'Meaning?'

'How come you've survived to this age without being strangled? You're driving me crazy…you think you know everything and even if you do, there's no need to share it.' Betsy tilted up her chin. 'For your information, I have a degree in business and the only advice I will require in that field is my own.'

Having delivered that news, Betsy stalked across the sand into the house. She was in the bedroom when Cristos strode in. He stilled behind her and before she could even guess his intention he had skimmed down the bikini straps on her slight shoulders so that the amount of sunlight her skin had absorbed could be clearly seen in the contrast.

Betsy squirmed and groaned out loud in frustration as she sat down at the foot of the bed. 'Just because you're right…it doesn't make me like you any better.'

Cristos strode into the bathroom and reappeared thirty seconds later with a bottle of lotion. He dropped it on the bed beside her. 'Apply this now and maybe you won't be doing a lobster impression by this evening.'

Betsy collided with brilliant dark eyes and her tummy took a hop, skip and a jump like an over-excited child about to climb on a big dipper. She twisted her head round, denying herself temptation, and directed her attention at the mirror again. Cristos sank down on the bed behind her and infiltrated her reflection as well. He looked so devastatingly handsome that she just stared, soft lips parting, mouth running dry.

'Stop looking at me like that...' Cristos advised, reaching for the bottle.

'You've got to be used to it by now.'

At that crack, the faintest hint of colour accentuated his arrogant cheekbones and she was amused. Of course he was aware that he was drop-dead gorgeous. Nobody possessed of his looks, height and superb build could remain ignorant of his own immense appeal.

'In fact not only are you used to the effect you create, you use it shamelessly to get your own way,' Betsy added for good measure.

'I don't usually have much of a problem getting my own way,' Cristos admitted without an ounce of discomfiture. 'Lecture over yet?'

As Betsy stiffened cool fingers smoothed soothing liquid across the hot skin on her shoulders and a tiny startled moan of sound broke from between her lips.

'Am I hurting you?' Cristos asked lazily.

'No...' If anyone had told Betsy that some day the touch of a man's hand on her shoulder would set her alight like a match dropped on a bale of hay, she would have laughed out loud. But the confident caress of his lean fingers was somehow making her unbearably aware of her own body in a way that made it almost impossible for her to stay still.

'Should I stop?' he husked.

'No...' She could not bear the idea of denying herself that physical contact. A kernel of heat was unfurling low in her pelvis. She was tempted to lean back into the hard, masculine strength of his powerful body. Shaken by the very thought of such behaviour, she went rigid. Desire was in her like a secret agent programmed to seek out her vulnerability. She looked back in the mirror to see Cristos even though she knew she should not. Her heartbeat thudded heavily inside her tight chest.

She thought of all the safe choices she had made and so many of them had been mistakes. All her life she had erred on the side of caution. She had wanted to train as a mechanic but instead she had spent three years at university studying for a career she had no interest in. For a year after that she had worked endless overtime in an office job she'd loathed and her lucrative salary had been of no comfort. In the same way she had been protecting herself from potential hurt when she'd held back from sleeping with Rory. She had always selected the most sensible and least risky option available...and Cristos was a high-risk heartbreaker.

In her mind's eye she pictured herself swivelling round on the mattress and moulding her lips to that wide, sensual mouth of his. She was shattered by just how fiercely she longed for that image to be true.

Taking her by surprise, Cristos rose upright in a fluid motion. He strolled into the bathroom to rinse his hands and murmured levelly, 'Take a break. I'm a lot more used to this heat than you are.'

But very unused to suppressing his libido around a beautiful woman, he conceded inwardly. He raked long fingers roughly through his cropped black hair but still he could see the slender elegant sweep of her back, the fairness of her colouring against his own and the incredibly feminine silky feel of her soft skin. He was becoming obsessed, he told himself angrily. He fed the fire with fierce concentration and then stacked wood.

Betsy regarded sex as something serious and he had never regarded sex as serious. But in the back of his mind lurked a vague and unsettling recollection of the much more conservative views of his mother, Calliope, who had died when he was eleven years old. To combat the rampant sexism of the male contingent of the Stephanides family, his mother had even then been talking to her son about stuff like respect, fidelity and self-discipline. And love. His lean, handsome face clenched hard. Well, suffice it to say that Calliope, who had married her true love at eighteen, had been very naïve on that score.

Betsy was, however, in a class of her own. From the minute she had admitted that she was a virgin Cristos had been forced to reassess his attitude to her. No longer could he stick her in the same category as the countless forgettable women who were pretty much willing to spread their legs for any rich man. But her very exclusivity made her an even more potent symbol of desire to a male who had always regarded the best things in life as being his...

CHAPTER FOUR

WHEN Betsy wakened, she could hardly credit that it was after one in the afternoon. She felt hugely guilty about her sloth. From the window she could see that Cristos was still up on the headland working and what had she been doing? Sleeping!

Hot and sticky, she stripped off the bikini, freshened up and put on the colourful halter-neck beach dress instead. She wouldn't let herself glance in the mirror and get embarrassed about how noticeably tiny her breasts would look shorn of a bra and how very thin and giraffe like her legs appeared in too short a skirt. Instead she washed out the bikini, draped it on the rear terrace to dry and busied herself making lunch.

Were her family climbing the walls with worry about her? She winced. There was no point agonising over what could not be helped. But for how long were they likely to be living on the island? Earlier that day, Cristos had brought her up to speed on the food and fuel levels at the house, which typically he had already checked out and considered in depth. They had ample supplies. Although the fresh food would eventually run out, the freezer was packed. There was also plenty of fuel to keep the generator ticking over.

She would have liked to ask Cristos how his grandfather was likely to react to a ransom demand for his grandson's release. So far she had held her tongue on the topic because anything relating to the kidnapping seemed to send Cristos through the roof and awaken all his dark suspicions about her having crime connections. In any case, how could Cristos really know how his elderly grandfather might react?

She walked out to the front of the house to call Cristos but there was no sign of him. Then she saw the heap of clothes on the sand and his seal-wet dark head gleaming as he cleaved through the sunlit waves out in the bay. Even though he was a powerful swimmer, she could not stop thinking about scary stuff like undertow. With considerable relief she watched him heading for shore again and standing up to wade through the last few feet of surf. At that point she received her very first view of a naked adult male.

In dismay, Betsy retreated back into the house. But that sight of Cristos unclothed was stamped in immoveable stone within her memory. He was magnificent: wide bronzed shoulders, powerful pectoral muscles accentuated by damp black curls, a sleek six pack torso and the narrow hips and long, powerful hair-roughened thighs of a male in the physical peak of condition. She blacked out any recollection of the more intimate part of him with puritanical thoroughness. After all, she was not a voyeur. She would give him five minutes to get his clothes on.

But when she went back onto the beach, Cristos was showering at the outside faucet and still naked as the day he had been born. Thoroughly fed up with his relaxed attitude to nudity, she backed off well out of view and yelled at the top of her voice, 'Lunch!'

She was standing with folded arms under the tree when Cristos finally came strolling towards her bare chested and barefoot, his chinos riding low on his lean hips, his shirt thrown over one shoulder. Dazzling dark eyes sought hers and a slow, lethal smile began to tug at the edges of his beautifully sculpted and highly expressive mouth.

That fast Betsy appreciated that he knew he had been seen and she turned a beetroot colour as far as her hairline. But, outraged as she was by his sheer insouciance, she still couldn't take her eyes off him. When he smiled her heartbeat went haywire and her mouth ran dry.

'You're so shy…it turns me on,' Cristos confided without shame.

'You must be hungry.' Betsy struggled to keep the lid on her responses to him by falling back on the prosaic.

'Right now…my only hunger is for you…' Smouldering golden eyes met hers with provocative force.

'You shouldn't be saying th-things like that to me,' she stammered, taken aback by his boldness.

Cristos helped himself to a glass of iced water from the table and drank thirstily. 'I want you, *pethi mou*. There's no shame in the truth.'

Entrapped, Betsy stared back at him and then painfully slowly she enforced her own will and disconnected from his stunning gaze to let her eyes drop. Only then did she notice what the taut fit of fabric straining over his groin could not conceal: he was fiercely aroused. Shock thrilled through her at that visible proof of his desire. Something that had repelled her in other men had a very different effect on her when it was Cristos in the starring role. She discovered that she was indecently fascinated and had to tear her attention from him.

'If you expect me to stop wanting you, go hide under a blanket,' Cristos advised.

'I am by no stretch of the imagination *that* fanciable!' Betsy shot back at him in angry embarrassment.

'You're so beautiful that I'm breaking my own rules and chasing a chauffeur,' Cristos informed her drily. 'You stopped *me* in my tracks and I don't mind admitting that when it comes to gorgeous women, I'm a connoisseur.'

Against her own will, she was captivated and madly curious. 'Have there been a lot of women in your life?'

Cristos nodded in silent confirmation.

'You *really* think I'm beautiful?'

Cristos read the anxious defensive look on her lovely face and wondered who was responsible for giving her such low self-esteem. 'You take my breath away,' he told her softly.

Her vulnerability touched him. She was so unlike the confident, conceited beauties that provided sexual entertainment in his leisure hours. Polished to the edges of their perfect nails, those women were as tough and cynical as he was. They traded their bodies for thrills, for status and for money. But neither his wealth nor his power had impressed Betsy. She was quite happy to shout at him and slap him and treat him as no other woman had ever dared. Was that why he found her such a distraction? Novelty value? Satisfied with that explanation, he closed the distance between them and pulled her into his arms with easy strength and unquestioning assurance.

In contact with the heat and solidarity of his big, powerful frame, Betsy trembled. *You take my breath away.* No man had ever said anything like that to her and it made her feel like a million dollars. She knew she ought to back off. She knew that she was dicing with danger and, in her mother's time-honoured phrase, asking for trouble. But when she looked up at Cristos and he held her close, she also knew that she would dig ditches and give at least ten years of her life to stay in his arms.

'You can kiss me…' she framed shakily.

A decent guy would walk away, Cristos reflected, forcing himself not to grab the opportunity with his usual immediacy. She was a virgin. He would be taking advantage. He did it in business all the time and never hesitated. What was the matter with him? He could make her first time special. Better him and his expertise than some drunken clumsy clod, who might string her a line and hurt her.

'I won't stop at kissing…' Cristos growled in hungry warning.

At that promise, a delicious little quiver shimmied down her spine, slivered through her belly and lodged low there in a burgeoning nest of warmth. She pushed her face into a powerful masculine shoulder, nostrils flaring on the sun warmed scent of him. She was utterly dizzy with longing and felt weak as a kitten. 'I feel all shaky,' she mumbled with a self-conscious laugh. 'What's wrong with me?'

He lifted her up into his arms and strode indoors. The shutters in the bedroom were half closed on the heat of the day. He laid her on the bed where an arrowing shaft of bright light flamed over her coppery mane of hair.

'Er…' Feeling hugely awkward and in shock in many ways at her own behaviour, Betsy cleared her throat. 'No-one in your life is going to be hurt by us getting together?' she queried, having belatedly appreciated that she had never actually asked if he was single.

'Nobody…' Cristos reached down to catch her hands in his and raise her up again.

Meshing long fingers into her wonderful hair, he brought his mouth down with passionate savagery on hers. His tongue darted in a searching foray between her readily parted lips and she jerked in eager response, locking her arms round his neck to imprison him. As he plundered her mouth with an erotic finesse that mimicked a much more sexual invasion, she shivered with response. When he lifted his handsome dark head again to let her breathe, being denied continuing contact with him was an actual pain.

'I was planning to teach you to swim this afternoon,' Cristos confided huskily. 'But now I'll teach you something infinitely more enjoyable.'

Barely able to credit that she had reached such a major decision without even thinking it through, Betsy wondered if there had always been a brazen hussy hiding inside her and waiting for her chance. 'I bet I'm useless at this…'-

'But no way am I,' Cristos teased with bred-in-the-bone assurance.

Reaching behind her, he deftly undid the halter tie at the nape of her neck. She sucked in a dismayed breath and shut her eyes tight. The mere thought of baring her body for the first time froze her to the spot. She was *so* skinny. Her sister had had more of a bust at thirteen than Betsy had as a grown-up and Gemma still liked to show off her lush curves in tight tops and low necklines. He would be disappointed. Of course he would be.

'Open your eyes…' Cristos urged thickly. 'I wouldn't like you to get a fright when I throw you on the bed and ravish you.'

Her lashes shot up on startled green eyes.

His glorious smile slashing his lean dark features, Cristos sank down on the side of the bed and pulled her down onto his lap. He tugged the dress down inch by inch until it fell free of the weight of her long hair and tumbled. At the point of total exposure, she stopped breathing altogether. He prevented her from leaning forward in a concealing movement, brushed her hair out of his way and bent her back over one arm to get the full effect of the petite pouting swells adorned by delicate rosy nipples. He exhaled audibly.

'Exquisite…' he pronounced raggedly, his devouring appraisal and the roughened note in his rich, dark drawl convincing proof of his genuine appreciation.

He cupped one breast and toyed with the sweet, succulent crest until it was swollen and stiff. She squirmed on his thighs, the warm, achy feeling low in her belly making her restive. He employed his mouth on her tender nipples, tasting and teasing until she moaned out loud and dug impatient fingers into his luxuriant black hair to drag his head up and find his gorgeous mouth for herself again.

'Cristos…?'

'Let's get comfortable…' Pulling free, Cristos settled her back against the pillows. He closed his hands into the hem of her dress and whisked it from round her hips to toss it aside. Clad only in the rather daring cerise lace thong she had found in a drawer with other equally adventurous panties, Betsy felt horribly naked and exposed. Angling back from her in a lithe movement, Cristos sprang upright.

'I can't believe I'm doing this,' she confided jaggedly, green eyes bright with bemusement.

'You haven't done anything yet.' Cristos slid the

bedspread out from beneath her and cast it in a spill of silk across the padded seat at the foot of the bed.

But nor had she thought about what she was about to do, Betsy conceded shamefacedly. Going to bed with Cristos and surrendering her virginity had been concepts that took her by storm, not the reasoned calm decisions that were the norm for her. For goodness' sake, she was twenty-five years old and still keen on a man who belonged to her sister, she reminded herself guiltily. Why shouldn't she settle for a passionate affair? Cristos could turn her inside out with one smile and make her knees go weak with one kiss. He mesmerised her and it might be juvenile of her to get caught up in such a physical infatuation but at least she wasn't kidding herself that it was anything more.

Cristos ran down the zip on his chinos and then stilled, ebony brows drawing together in a frown. 'Are you willing to run the risk that I could get you pregnant?'

Betsy froze.

Cristos groaned out loud. 'I know…you forgot about that aspect. So did I. I can't believe that I almost overlooked an issue of that gravity but, for some crazy reason, I don't think straight around you.'

Betsy was very pale. She hugged her knees to her breasts. 'We can't do this…I would die if I got pregnant—'

Cristos winced. 'Don't be such a pessimist. I'll be careful…I'll withdraw.'

Betsy had turned very pink at that declaration and she was no longer meeting his brilliant dark gaze. 'It's too risky—'

'I'm a risk-taker—'

'I'm not, never have been.'

'If I get you pregnant I will be there for you every step of the way,' Cristos swore huskily. 'You don't need to worry. I don't think it's going to happen, but be assured that if it does I will take full responsibility and support you.'

Betsy stole a glance at his devastatingly handsome face. Was he really thinking things through? She could not help being impressed.

'Trust me, *pethi mou…*' Cristos added, doffing his chinos with a flourish.

His designer boxers interfered with her concentration. He shed those too with the natural grace that accompanied every supple movement of his lean, hard body. Involuntarily she stared at the rigid maleness of his bold shaft and hastily averted her eyes, thinking that she had just found another very good reason why they should not be getting together. In fact she was having very serious second thoughts.

'It's not that I don't trust you,' she began tremulously as the mattress sank beneath his weight. 'It's just that—'

'You're nervous and outrageously shy about displaying your fantastic figure.' Cristos parted her arms, spread them wide and rearranged her hair so that the tumbled strands no longer concealed her breasts. 'I'm your perfect match. I don't have a modest bone in my entire body.'

'I know that but…' Betsy looked up at him and met scorching golden eyes that sent her heartbeat into a sprint.

'All you have to do is lie back and enjoy being seduced,' Cristos told her lazily, tipping her back so that her mane of hair spread in a vibrant fan across the pillows. 'I had several wildly erotic dreams about you before we even met on Friday. Now I have you here on this bed I intend to live the fantasy.'

'I'm not a fantasy, though,' she whispered. 'I'm just an ordinary woman.'

'No ordinary woman could exercise this much sexual power over me…I'm a tough guy to pull,' Cristos asserted, holding her hands down beneath his and feeding from the sweetness of her already-reddened mouth with burning intensity.

It was as if every skin cell in her body were throbbing into new life. He let his teeth graze her throat and her pulses leapt with almost painful enthusiasm. Electric excitement had her in its grip. His thumbs flicked over her distended nipples, lingered to torment. Even more sensitive there than she had been minutes earlier, a whimper of sound escaped her. Her hips were shifting on the cool sheet below her. A barely understood hunger was tearing at her in waves of wanting. She was unprepared for the sharp bittersweet edge of sensation that bereft her of control, leaving her capable only of yearning for the next and the next. But, somehow, not the most passionate kiss or knowing caress could answer the fever burning inside her.

'I didn't know it would be like this…' she gasped, both exhilarated and scared by the sheer overwhelming force of her own longing.

'Layer on layer of the most perfect pleasure, *pethi mou*.'

He skimmed through the silken copper curls below her belly and lightly traced the thrumming heart of her. She was unbearably tender, hot and damp. She twisted. He held her still. He let his mouth trail a slow, soothing passage down over her quivering body. 'Relax…'

She was boneless with anticipation. Her hands fluttered over him, discovering the bunched muscles of his shoulders, the smooth hard strength of his back. The feel of his incredibly male body against hers held her rapt. The taste of his skin beneath her lips and her tongue enchanted her. She was in a world of discovery. He explored the slick wet heat of her. She twisted and turned, the fire of her desire racing higher and higher until it threatened to consume her.

He tilted her back and shifted over her to ease into her tight, moist entrance degree by degree. Her eyes opened wide in wonderment. Where she had ached he filled her to the hilt. The sudden stark flash of pain as he powered through the barrier of her resisting flesh took her by surprise and then he thrust into her some more.

Cristos looked down at her with hot golden eyes. 'You feel awesome.'

He eased his hands beneath her hips, arched her up to him and sank even deeper into her with a groan of very male satisfaction. She had no time to catch her breath. With slow, provocative deliberation, he set a sensual rhythm that made her heart pound like mad against her breastbone. He ground down into her and wild excitement seized her. The pace quickened. She moved against him with an abandon that became more and more frenzied. Any notion of control was long gone. She was reaching for the very zenith of pleasure when without any warning he suddenly yanked himself back from her.

'Cristos…?' she yelped in disbelief and she stretched up and hauled him back to her before he could complete his withdrawal.

He slammed back into her with welcome fervour. She hit the heights in an explosion of ecstasy. He bit out something raw in his own language. His magnificent body shuddered over her and she clung to him as the shattering pagan surge of pleasure rocked them both.

In the aftermath, she hugged him close, revelling in that new intimacy and feeling incredibly content.

'As withdrawals go, that was a disaster,' Cristos muttered breathlessly, surveying her nonetheless with scorching golden eyes of appreciation and smoothing back her tousled hair to drop a kiss on her brow.

'Oh…' Too late, Betsy realised what she had done and she blamed her own mindless excitement for her lack of awareness. 'My fault.'

'But as an experience…it was the ultimate. I do hope this isn't going to be a one-night stand,' Cristos murmured teasingly, flipping over onto his back and scooping her up to arrange her back on top of him.

In rather a daze at the new state of play between them, Betsy gazed down at him. Feeling quite unlike herself and insanely happy, she smiled.

The softened light in her clear eyes disturbed Cristos. 'A word of warning,' he murmured lightly. 'Don't go falling in love with me. I'm not into all that.'

A deep inner chill banished her sunny mood. It took effort not to betray her disconcertion and her hurt. It took even more of an effort to produce an amused laugh. 'You don't need to worry,' she told him, affronted by the warning he had considered it necessary to give her. 'I'm in love with someone else.'

Astonished by that careless statement, Cristos went very still. He did not think about what he did next; he went with his gut reaction. Clamping two hands to her waist, he scooped her off him again and dumped her back on the bed beside him with a scant lack of ceremony. 'Then why did you go to bed with me?'

Taken aback by his flagrant anger, Betsy scrambled out of the bed. Only then did she recall that she was stark naked and an immediate need to drop to her knees in search of something to wear could not have been said to cool her temper. Below the bed she found the sarong she had discarded earlier and she dragged it round herself.

'I'm *waiting* for an answer...' Cristos stressed.

'Well, I don't see what you have to get all worked up about.' Betsy's ire was up and she had gone on the defensive. 'When you felt the need to tell me not to go falling for you, you should be grateful to hear that I'm in love with another man!'

'Who is he?' Cristos growled, furious with her, aghast at her lack of shame. To think that he had fondly imagined that she was vulnerable, naïve...

'None of your business.' Betsy tied the sarong in a knot over her breasts. Her hands were all fingers and thumbs. She was upset and she couldn't understand why she had had such a violent adverse response to what he had said to her.

'You made it mine when you got into bed with me,' Cristos framed in a raw undertone. 'Who is this guy? Your boyfriend?'

Her resistance gave in the surge of bitterness that that enquiry produced. 'He was once,' she admitted tightly. 'But now he lives with my sister and they have a child.'

At that admission, the savage edge to his anger blunted. The other guy was unavailable and not a rival. 'How long since you were with him?'

'Three years.'

Cristos treated her to a derisive appraisal. 'And you *still* haven't got over him?'

'You are one hateful, sarcastic bastard when you want to be!' Betsy yelled at him full throttle, high spots of colour burning over her cheeks.

A symphony of bronzed flesh and powerful masculinity, Cristos lounged back against the tumbled pillows, offensive in his studied relaxation. 'Three years after this guy shacks up with your sister, you're still in love with him…don't *you* think that's more than a little sad?'

Betsy was in such a rage she felt light-headed. 'You don't understand what you're talking about. Rory was my best friend, my soul mate—'

'But you never screwed him,' Cristos slotted in with a blunt lack of respect for such high-flown sentiments that sent her hot temper climbing even higher. 'So he must have been a non-starter between the sheets.'

'You're disgusting…you reduce everything to a sexual level!' Betsy slammed back at him.

'I'm also the guy you gave your virginity to.'

'So you've got sex appeal …just as well, you've got nothing else!' Betsy slung at him between gritted teeth. 'You're insensitive, ignorant, vain—'

'Where the hell do you get off calling me vain?' Cristos roared at her.

Hands on her slender hips, Betsy treated him to an all-encompassing look of scorn such as he had never before received from a member of her sex. 'Suggesting that I would be thick enough to fall in love with a guy like you! And you don't think that's vain?'

Golden eyes flaming with fierce pride, Cristos sprang off the bed like a panther about to pounce on prey. 'Why wouldn't you fall in love with me?'

'It's nothing personal but you're not Rory,' Betsy told him brittly, horrified to recognise the prickling sensation behind her eyes and taking hurried refuge in the bathroom before she let herself down a bucketful.

Seething with frustration, incapable of letting the issue drop, Cristos knocked on the door. She ignored it. He opened the door. Tear-tracks marking her cheeks, she was wiping her eyes. His anger vanished. He closed his arms round her. 'This is insane. I don't even know what we're arguing about—'

'Your conviction that you're an intensely lovable person and fatally attractive to virgins,' Betsy countered somewhat snidely in punishment for his having caught her crying.

'It's the tension we're living with here…it had to find a vent somewhere,' Cristos asserted, disregarding that facetious comment.

Her rigidity gave and she collapsed into the sheltering warmth of his lean, powerful body. She didn't know why she had got so angry and distressed. She didn't know why he had a magical ability to make her so angry she was ready to explode. She didn't even know why she was ruder to him than she had ever been to anyone else. All she recognised at that instant was that she was confused, afraid of the disturbing strength of her own emotions and in dire need of comfort. She had not acknowledged that they were both stressed out and striving to make the best of a frightening situation they could not control. Cristos was like her. He didn't whinge.

Pulling her close, he scooped her up and carried her back to bed. 'You have three choices,' he murmured, stunning dark golden eyes entrapping her with charismatic ease. 'One…I give you some space.'

Betsy considered that and finally wrinkled her nose.

'Two…I give you your first swimming lesson.'

Betsy made a rather vulgar gagging sound, which made him grin with startled appreciation.

'Three…I get out the champagne, which is probably of vinegar vintage, and come back to bed.'

'Stuff the champagne,' she told him, but hot-cheeked at her own nerve she opened her arms. She wanted him. It was that simple. No need to make a production out of it, she told herself staunchly.

Five days later, Betsy flopped on the sand and punched a victory sign in the air. 'I can swim!'

'But you still don't go into the water on your own,' Cristos delivered.

Laughing, green eyes shining with mischief, she leant over him. 'Don't you ever get tired of ordering me about?'

'No, I really get off on it…' Cristos curled his fingers into the wet coil of her bright hair and dragged her down to him with the cool confidence of a male who knew that his attentions were always welcome. He captured her lips, conducted a sensual invasion that reduced her to shivering compliancy. His beautiful dark golden eyes flared over her with sensual intent and then he sat up, carrying her with him. 'I want you again, *pethi mou*.'

He took her into the cool of the bedroom. He had barely touched her but already her body was ready for him. She wanted him so badly she was trembling. He unclipped her bikini bra, baring her pert breasts. His roughened growl of pleasure broke the buzzing silence and she leant back against him with a low moan of encouragement while he stroked the distended pink nipples straining for his attention.

'You're so quiet with me now,' Cristos censured, pressing her back against the bed where she rested boneless, enslaved by him.

Her lashes lowered in concealment. What was there to say when she had to be careful not to betray herself? There was not a minute in the day when she did not think of him. Initial fascination and attraction had melded into a much more dangerous obsession. She had begun admiring the flip side of his arrogant temperament: his courage, his uncompromising strength of character and intelligence. Before she knew where she was, she had found herself lying in eager wait for his wonderful smile. In spite of all her proud assurances to the contrary, she had fallen headlong and hopelessly in love with Cristos Stephanides.

'But even your silence excites me,' Cristos confided, tugging up her shapely knees to remove her bikini pants. 'It gives me a high when you cry out with pleasure…'

He parted the damp petals of her womanhood to find the most sensitive spot of all and suddenly she was all heat and desperate need. But where she most ached for him, he touched her not at all. In a process of sensual torment he took her to a peak again and again, always denying her the fulfilment she craved. She writhed in frustration, whimpered in protest. Only when he was satisfied that she had reached the very edge of extreme arousal did he turn her over and plunge into the tender heart of her with a devastating expertise that sent her into an instantaneous and wildly exciting climax.

Afterwards, he curled her slender, exhausted body

up against him and surveyed her with immense satisfaction. Sex with her was incredible but he would not have dreamt of telling her that. He could not get enough of her. He would not have told her that even under torture. He lifted her hand and planted a kiss in the centre of her palm. He wrapped his arms round her, submitted with only a very slight wince to being hugged for the first time since his childhood. He knew what she liked. He knew how to keep her happy. In return for unlimited sex, and moreover the best sex he had ever had, he made a very real effort to be affectionate. Why? He had already decided that when they got off the island he would keep her in his life as his mistress. After all, he had moulded her into exactly what he wanted.

When Betsy emerged from the bathroom towelling her hair dry, she found herself alone again. Cristos would be checking the fire on the headland. He was impossibly energetic from dawn to midnight and she struggled to keep up with him. The old boathouse was piled high with junk and he was using it to keep the signal fire alight. So far, the fire had failed to attract attention. But then, since they had not even seen a fishing boat, it was clear that the island did not lie close to the shipping lanes. With stones they had picked out a giant SOS on the beach that could be seen from the air, but they had yet to see a single small plane of the type that would fly low enough to read their message.

It was very hot but Betsy was determined to do her share of the heavy work. She padded into the shadowy depths of the boathouse and swept up a dusty old cardboard box. Through the torn lid she could see magazines. She would cart it up to feed the fire. It was a steep climb and when she got there Cristos was no-where to be seen. She espied him down on the beach. The fire was low and she settled the box hurriedly on top of it, reasoning that it would burn slower and last longer as fuel that way.

She had reached the dunes below when a whistling, hissing sound followed by an explosive bang brought her to an astonished halt. The seeming equivalent of a very violent firework torched through the clear blue sky above and her jaw dropped.

'Why didn't you tell me you'd found a flare? Why the hell did you just throw it on the fire?' Cristos shouted at her from about thirty feet away, his lean, darkly handsome face hard with incredulity.

Another flare shot up over the headland in a fierce bright rocket of flame and a shower of sparks. Paralysed to the spot, and it was a paralysis that Cristos seemed to share, she watched in horror as a pyrotechnic display of flares fired off in all directions. In all six had exploded and of those only one failed to make the ascent into the sky.

'I didn't know there were flares. I took the box out of the boathouse. I thought it was full of maga-zines...that was all I could see!' Betsy admitted in consternation.

Glittering dark eyes pinned to her in angry condem-nation, Cristos spread his lean brown hands wide. 'You put the box on the fire without checking the con-tents?'

Stiff with guilt, she nodded.

'Those flares would have had a much greater chance of being noticed at night. Thanks to your carelessness, they've been wasted!' Cristos derided.

'I thought you'd already searched through everything in the boathouse!' Betsy protested and, sidestepping him, she headed off, eyes stinging at the awful fear that she might have blown their best chance for getting off the island.

When Cristos was annoyed with her, a knot of pain formed inside Betsy and she started feeling as if she had lost a whole layer of protective skin. But in truth, she recognised ruefully, what she had lost was her independence and her peace of mind. She judged herself through his eyes. His opinions mattered. He had imposed his powerful personality on her whether she liked it or not. Her time with him had also taught her a lot about herself. The love she had honestly believed she still cherished for Rory had been composed of nothing more than fondness and her reluctance to let go of her sentimental links to the past.

Late afternoon, Cristos strode into the house and pulled her into his arms, impervious to the ice signals she was handing out. They were both hot-tempered. It was a scene that had occurred between them on several occasions. He would never discuss the argument. He would simply pretend it had not happened and even while she was soothed by the speed with which he always healed a breach that arrogant refusal to acknowledge their differences drove her crazy. But this time she had no opportunity to quibble about the silent terms of reconciliation. He kissed her with hard, hungry urgency.

Taken aback, she had no time even to catch her breath before Cristos, emanating tightly leashed emotions in a force field that she could feel, his dark eyes bright with satisfaction, turned her to the window so that she could see the blue and white fishing boat tied up at the jetty. 'We've been rescued...'

Everything from that point went at supersonic speed. The distress flares had brought the young fisherman to investigate. Within ten minutes, Betsy was being helped into the boat, still colourfully clothed in a sundress and bikini pants, her crumpled uniform stuffed in a carrier bag. While she watched the island recede into the purplish haze of ever greater distance, Cristos was talking in voluble Greek into the radio in the wheelhouse.

'Your family will be informed that you are safe,' Cristos assured her in an aside when she hovered nearby. 'My grandfather will organise everything.'

For all the fact that they had their freedom back, Betsy felt superfluous to requirements and oddly empty and scared. Even so she did not want to hang round Cristos like a limpet. When they were within sight of land again, she asked him if he had found out the name of the island they had been on.

'Why would you be interested?' he asked, his surprise palpable, but he spoke to the fisherman.

'Mos…it's called. We're in the Cyclades,' he added.

They landed on the island of Sifnos, which was as gloriously green in its spring splendour as Mos had been. Again she was left alone while Cristos went off to make use of the private phone offered to him. She did not like to ask if she could accompany him and it was thirty minutes before he reappeared, his bold bronzed features grave.

'Did the kidnappers ask for a ransom? Did you find out *anything* about them?' she prompted then, desperate for a little information. She was feeling shut out and excluded. Cristos was back in his own world, she conceded, and already he was acting cool and detached. What they had shared on the island might as well have taken place on another planet, she thought fearfully.

His lean, strong face was expressionless. 'Nothing…but transport to take us back to the mainland should be arriving very soon.'

'I have no passport…how am I going to travel home?'

'Your embassy has been informed. They will take care of that.'

'When are the police going to question us?'

Cristos shrugged. He did not know what to say to her. He had been shattered by what he had just learned from his grandfather and he was still in shock. Spyros, his own cousin, had had him kidnapped. Cristos was outraged but also ashamed that one of his own kin could have sunk so low with only greed as an excuse. And if Patras Stephanides had anything to do with it, there would be no further investigation of his grandson's brief disappearance for it was not as though charges could be brought against those responsible.

Five days ago, Spyros and his partners in crime, Joe Tyler and two other men, had all been killed when the helicopter that Spyros had been piloting had crashed in the Aegean sea on the way back from Mos. Nothing would be gained from revealing the truth to Betsy or to anybody else. Indeed the honour of the Stephanides name and Spyros' grieving family required the protection of silence.

As the silence stretched Betsy stiffened.

Dark eyes grim, Cristos breathed in deep. 'There is something I should tell you…I'm engaged. My fiancée will be waiting to greet me in Athens, so we will be travelling separately.'

His words, for in no way could she have described that statement as either apologetic or confessional, hit her like a brick smashing through a window. In that moment everything changed and everything she had shared with him took on a far different aspect. She walked away a few steps to stare blindly out at the picturesque harbour. For long, timeless minutes she struggled to deal with the greatest pain she had ever known.

'You lied to me,' she said.

'I did not.'

'I asked you if anyone in your life would be hurt by us being together and you said no,' she reminded him in a shaking undertone while she fought not to lose her temper or cry or indeed do anything that might reveal to him just how badly she was hurting.

'I answered truthfully. Petrina does not interfere. She is not concerned by my fidelity but I respect her position and I am always discreet.'

Hatred and bitterness threatened to spread like a pool of poison inside Betsy. She hugged her arms round herself, striving to contain her tempestuous emotions.

'I want you to remain part of my life…'

An incredulous laugh empty of humour was wrenched from her and she moved away another step, terrified that she might break down into tears. 'You've got to be joking.'

'I won't give you up, *pethi mou*,' Cristos breathed, pale with tension beneath his olive skin, glittering dark eyes intently pinned to her every change of expression. 'Nothing is perfect. But you can still be with me.'

'You think I want you so much that I'd be prepared to share you?' Eyes witch-green with rampant loathing, Betsy rounded on him like a tigress. 'Go take a running jump, Cristos!'

CHAPTER FIVE

BETSY lifted the phone and heard the broken dialling tone that let her know that she had messages to collect on the answering service.

She listened to her messages. Cristos three times over: Cristos angry, angrier and even more angry. Cristos, who could not believe or accept that she would not speak to him. He was amazingly persistent and unbelievably stubborn in the face of repeated rejection. The guy whom she had believed was so special. The guy who had taken gross advantage of her naïve trust. She blamed herself more than she blamed him, though. Had ever a woman contributed more to her own downfall?

Cristos had only been interested in sex. Cristos had not even pretended that he was interested in anything else. A small example of that reality was that, in spite of spending virtually every waking hour with her for the best part of a week, Cristos had still never got around to asking her what sort of a business she hoped to start up. He had been careful to keep things unemotional and impersonal on his side of the fence, but she had got far, far too personal when she'd fallen in love with him.

It was only three weeks since she had returned from Greece. Her life had been turned upside down. She couldn't sleep, had lost interest in eating and had to drag herself out of bed in the morning. She felt like a fake person running round behind a plastic smile.

Inside herself she was hollow with misery and aloneness. But on the face of it, her life was virtually the same as it had ever been.

The kidnapping had been hushed up. Why, she had no idea, but she suspected that there might be a lot of truth in that phrase, 'money talks.' A Stephanides lawyer had met her when she'd landed in Athens. He had assisted her through the process of proving her identity and getting herself home. He had also informed her of the helicopter crash, which had taken the life of Joe Tyler and the men with him. She had returned to work to discover that the limo she had crashed had already been repaired. Her boss had been advised to keep the matter quiet and inform the curious that she had gone off on a last-minute holiday. The Stephanides family had gone to considerable lengths to cover up the evidence that a crime had been committed.

In an effort to distract herself from her unhappiness, Betsy had decided it was time she took the plunge and focused her energies on opening up a garage specialising in classic car restoration. It was two years now since her grandfather had died and his estate had been divided between Betsy and Gemma. With a healthy savings account, Betsy knew the chances were good that the bank would give her a loan.

Yet she had still not made that all-important appointment at the bank. Why? Her period was a few days late and she was terrified that Cristos might have got her pregnant. Yet she had still not worked up the courage to go and buy a pregnancy test because she was praying that fear was making her fanciful. After all, Cristos had been reasonably careful. She blocked out an uneasy recollection of the passion that had led to one or two oversights. Furthermore, Cristos had checked on the dates of her menstrual cycle and, while freely admitting that he had never made such calculations in his life, he had been of the opinion that they were really safe from repercussions…

Betsy was in the anxious act of wondering whether her vanished appetite might relate to more than a broken heart when a knock sounded on the door of her bedsit. It was Rory and she was really surprised: in all the years since they had broken up and he had set up home with her sister, he had never come to visit her. His blue eyes were red-rimmed with tiredness and his smart suit was crumpled. Once she had believed he was pretty attractive. Now, she registered that to her he just looked ordinary.

'What's up?' she asked. 'Is Gemma ill?'

'We've split up…'

Eyes rounding in disbelief, Betsy stilled. 'You're not serious?'

'I thought you'd be the last to know.' Rory grimaced. 'But *I* don't have anything to hide. I moved out yesterday.'

Betsy was shocked and could not think of how best to greet such an announcement from Rory. In truth, she just wanted him to disappear into thin air. His very presence on her doorstep meant trouble. Gemma would throw a fit if she found out that her boyfriend had gone to visit her sister and Betsy had no desire to get involved in the fallout. 'That's awful…I'm sorry,' she said stiltedly. 'But hopefully it's just a temporary blip—'

'It's no blip,' Rory informed her heavily. 'Your sister has another man. Aren't you going to invite me in?'

Trying to look more welcoming, Betsy stood back. 'There's got to have been a misunderstanding, Rory.'

'No, he's her boss and he's married. All the evenings that Gemma was supposed to be going to her fitness class she was actually with *him*. Do you know how I found out?' Rory prompted bitterly. 'The night your parents were told you'd been kidnapped they came round to our apartment and I rushed out to the college to fetch Gemma home early. The teacher hadn't seen her since last term!'

Betsy tried not to wince. 'Gemma would hate you telling me this stuff—' Her doorbell buzzed and, highly relieved by the interruption, she went to answer it, praying that Rory would take the hint and leave.

It was Cristos. The unexpected sight of him welded her to the spot. Sheathed in a caramel-coloured suit that shrieked designer tailoring, he was taller, broader, darker, and altogether more gorgeous than she had allowed herself to remember and, like a foodaholic on the edge of starvation, she couldn't stop staring. His stunning dark golden eyes met hers in an almost physical collision.

'I must talk to you…who's that behind you?' Cristos suddenly shot at her rawly, striding forward and setting her bodily out of his path to confront Rory. 'Who are you?'

Totally unprepared for his hostile behaviour, Betsy spun round in bewilderment. 'This is my sister's boyfriend, Rory.'

'What the hell are you doing here?' Cristos growled, hands clenching into fists, rage rolling up through him like volcanic lava seeking a vent. Rory, the guy she said she loved, here alone with her. While he was being treated like the plague for being engaged, Betsy was entertaining—in a room with a bed in it—the louse who had cheated on her with her own sister. Where was the justice in that?

Dwarfed by Cristos in size and never having been the physical type, Rory backed up against the wall. 'Betsy and I are good friends.'

Without the slightest warning of the aggression to come, Cristos closed two powerful hands into Rory's jacket and lifted him right off his feet. 'You're no friend. I saw the way you look at her and I'm a possessive man. I don't want you near her. Is that understood?'

'Have you gone mad?' Betsy screeched in horror at the scene before her and hauled unavailingly at Cristos' suit jacket. 'Let go of him!'

'Drop me...preferably all in one piece,' Rory advised drily, but his complexion was as colourless as the white-painted wall behind him.

'Cristos!' Betsy exclaimed fiercely.

Cristos lowered the smaller man to the floor again, backed off a step, twitched his cuffs straight while hoping that his target would do the manly thing and take a swing at him.

'I could have you charged with assault,' Rory informed him instead, straightening his tie.

Disappointed, Cristos thrust the door wider. 'Get out...'

Trembling, Betsy gulped in a sustaining breath. She was appalled by Cristos' conduct. Rory hovered, visibly keen to be gone but reluctant to back down in front of another man.

'I'll be fine...it'll be better if you leave.' She was quick to give Rory his escape clause.

Cristos stood at the window. He was thrown by his

own loss of control and shaken by his very sincere desire to hammer Rory to a pulp. He prided himself on his self-discipline. He could not understand what was wrong with him. Nothing had felt right since he'd returned home and all too many things roused him to impatience and annoyance.

His grandfather, Patras, had been blunt. 'You're like an angry bear looking for a fight. When you walk into a room, I feel I should take cover. What happened to you on that island?'

'I want you to leave…I'm not talking to you,' Betsy said doggedly, breaking into his ruminations.

Cristos devoured her in a long, lingering scrutiny. She had lost weight. Her eyes looked too big for her pale face. Her jeans and shirt were downright drab. But she was one of those rare women whose pure natural beauty would always outshine any frame and any physical flaw. Her unhappiness was also as apparent to him as his own seething frustration. 'What was Mr Sad doing here with you?'

An embarrassed flush lit Betsy's cheeks. On the island, Cristos had got chapter and verse on Rory's transfer of affections to Gemma out of her. It was, when she thought about it, the only personal topic he had pursued with the slightest interest.

'Rory and Gemma are having problems…he wanted someone to talk to—'

'I shouldn't think their problems will be solved by your personal intervention,' Cristos spelt out with contemptuous clarity.

'You're misjudging me,' Betsy murmured tightly, but ironically she was content for him to continue believing that she was still keen on Rory. While he believed that, he was unlikely to suspect the much more humiliating truth. 'And if you won't leave, I'm going out.'

'I want you to give me five minutes…that's all.' Cristos sought and held her evasive gaze and finally she jerked her chin in grudging agreement.

Restive as a jungle cat on the prowl, he paced across the room and, while he wasn't looking at her, she took the opportunity to feast her eyes on him. No matter how angry and bitter she was, she still craved him with every wretched fibre of her being.

Cristos spread fluid hands in a fatalistic arc. 'We're good together, *pethi mou*. I have missed you—'

'The sex…that's what you missed. You'll survive,' Betsy countered stonily.

'I miss your company almost as much. I have never said that to a woman before.' Cristos surveyed her as though he was expecting her to be so impressed she would pass out at his feet.

'You're engaged. You're not free to miss me.' Snatching up her fleece jacket and her keys, Betsy opened the door.

Cristos caught her hand in his. 'I won't quit…I *can't* quit. I want you. As my mistress, you would have everything.'

'Except the right to call you mine—'

'No woman has that privilege—'

'Except the right to walk down the street with you and be introduced to your friends as an equal.' Her voice had got thin and shrill and she was ashamed that she was actually answering him as if he had offered her a normal relationship.

What was normal about a guy who in all seriousness offered you the hallowed position of mistress in his life? And not in a tone of apology? He was spoilt rotten, she thought with fierce bitterness. So many women must have said yes to Cristos. His fiancée was equally to blame for giving him the freedom to do as he liked. He was rich, successful, breathtakingly handsome and fantastic in bed. Lots of women would bend the rules for him. A good few of those same women must have been as foolish as Betsy had been at the outset of their affair: quietly hopeful that his anti-love and -commitment warning was just defensive whitewash. She had learned the hard way that she was dealing with a cool and ruthless womaniser.

'Betsy…'

Betsy trailed her fingers free of his hold. 'Stop saying my name like it's something special because you treated me as if my feelings were of no account. I wasn't a person to you—'

Hard golden eyes challenged hers. 'That's untrue—'

'Then explain why you never even asked what type of business I was planning to set up? Classic car restoration, by the way! Or why I'm in the job I'm in. You cheated me too,' she condemned in fiery addition. 'I had the right to know that you were engaged to another woman. I would never have got mixed up with you if I'd known that—'

'*Theos mou…*' The merest hint of discomfited colour emphasising the sculpted slant of his superb cheekbones, Cristos vented an angry laugh of disagreement. 'Neither of us was able to fight the desire we felt for each other—'

'You didn't even *try*—'

'For your information, I walked away the first time I saw you,' Cristos reminded her furiously, lean, strong face taut. 'You were a chauffeur…do you really think I was keen to pull you when I realised that?'

'Oh, you patronising, snobbish jerk!' Enraged by that admission, Betsy stalked out onto the landing and headed down the stairs. 'Pull the door after you!' she called over her shoulder.

Above her the bedsit door slammed and Cristos strode in pursuit. 'I was not patronising you, I was being honest. Since when has it been a crime to be honest?' he demanded, following her out onto the street.

'It's a hanging offence when you've got no diplomacy and an exaggerated idea of your own importance!' Betsy launched back at full volume. 'And how dare you refer to yourself as honest? You were deliberately, sneakily, calculatingly secretive about the fact that you were engaged!'

Impervious to the fact that his bodyguards were open-mouthed with astonishment at the spectacle being acted out in front of them, Cristos drew level with Betsy. He was in a black fury that consumed all awareness of his surroundings. 'I won't phone you again,' he bit out.

'Promises…promises…' Betsy shot him a gleaming look of catlike provocation.

'I won't come here again either,' he gritted in a wrathful undertone. 'Next time you will come to me—'

'Only in your dreams!' she swore, stalking round the corner into the next street.

He was a step ahead of her. He splayed one hand against the wall to prevent her moving on and the other behind her. With an exaggerated sigh belied by the brightness of her gaze, she slumped back against the bricks. 'Haven't you had enough yet?' she asked, shamelessly, helplessly exhilarated by the cut and thrust of fighting with him.

'Nowhere near enough...' Scorching golden eyes assailed hers and the equivalent of an electric shock triggered inside her.

'Meaning?' Furious as she was with him, she was mesmerised.

Hands braced either side of her, he lowered his arrogant dark head and pried her lips apart in a kiss so hot she saw flames and sparks and inwardly burned.

Cristos lifted his head again, his stunning gaze radiating primal male satisfaction. 'I can wait, *pethi mou*. You'll come to me...'

Betsy walked on down the street on legs that were threatening to fold under her. She felt as if she were leaving part of herself behind. She also felt almost dizzy with rage. He was turning her into a split personality. She hated him but at the same time she craved him like an addictive drug. Furious tears prickled behind her eyes and she blinked them back, angry with herself for being so weak. She would get over him, she told herself. After all, she had managed to get over Rory without even noticing her achievement.

The following day, when Betsy finished work, she found Gemma waiting for her outside Imperial Limousines. Her sister had a tight defensive set to her pretty face that made Betsy's heart sink.

'Have you seen Rory?' Gemma asked stiffly.

Betsy very rarely told a lie but her backbone crumbled at the prospect of confessing that Rory had called round the night before. 'Why would I have?' she asked with what she hoped was a convincing show of surprise.

Gemma looked so relieved that Betsy knew that lying had been the right thing to do. Her sibling dragged her across the road into a bar and proceeded to tell all about her big bust-up with Rory. Unaccustomed to such a sisterly confessional, Betsy was nonetheless very pleased.

'I wanted to make him jealous because he's been taking me for granted. But of course I haven't been having an affair.' Gemma tossed her blonde head. 'I just wanted to light a fire under Rory.'

'Well, you've certainly done that.'

'He wasn't supposed to pack his bags and move out!' Gemma snapped. 'I got fed up with the evening class and started going off for a quick drink with a mate instead. Rory's had a thing about my boss ever since he saw me flirting with him at last year's Christmas do. We had a fight and I wanted to hurt him, so I let him think the worst.'

Betsy was feeling a little nauseous and preoccupied. 'Do you smell that perfume?' she whispered across the table. 'Isn't it overpowering? I swear it's making me feel sick.'

'It's not bothering me. But I was very sensitive to certain smells when I was carrying Sophie,' Gemma confided. 'Anyway, as I was saying, I was testing Rory—'

Betsy had paled at that casual reference to Gemma's pregnancy. 'Testing him?'

Gemma gave her a defiant look. 'He's never told me he loves me. But then he probably got fed up telling you and being treated like a doormat—'

Tired of being attacked, Betsy said, 'For goodness' sake—'

'You walked all over Rory! First you gave up that terrific job you had without even consulting him, then you signed up as a limo driver and then you told him you needed time to think about whether or not you wanted to marry him. You were much too bossy for him,' Gemma informed her smugly.

Betsy compressed her lips. It was an unfamiliar view of her relationship with Rory and, even if it did contain glimmerings of truth, Betsy was weary of the past being constantly rehashed. 'Haven't we moved on from all that yet?' she asked quietly. 'It is a long time ago.'

The rebuke made Gemma colour angrily. 'It's been no picnic for me following in your footsteps. Always feeling second-best, always wondering if he's only with me because of Sophie—'

'But Rory loves you,' Betsy countered levelly.

'He's never said so.'

'You can see it,' Betsy assured her.

'Honestly?' Her sister's face lit up and Betsy was surprised to appreciate just how insecure the younger woman still felt. Insecure and jealous, she saw for the first time. 'I think I'll ask him round to talk tonight…'

Soon after that, Gemma was about to take her leave when she began rustling in her handbag. 'I almost forgot. I thought you'd be interested in seeing this…'

'Seeing what?'

Gemma handed Betsy a magazine clipping that carried a photograph of Cristos dancing with a blonde woman. The blood drained from Betsy's face.

'I can't get over the fact that you never even *mentioned* that Cristos Stephanides is a mega-sexy hunk…' her sister was scolding.

Her stomach churning, Betsy read the inscription below the photo: 'Greek tycoon, Cristos Stephanides,

with his fiancée, heiress Petrina Rhodias, opening the
Stephanides charity ball in Athens.

'He's very good-looking—'

'Yeah,' Betsy cut in tightly, staring fixedly at
Petrina, a stunning Nordic blonde in a fabulous white
ballgown, diamonds sparkling at her throat. Talk about
being outclassed! The photo really said it all! Petrina
was Cristos' equal in looks, status and wealth. Betsy's
throat closed over and she snatched in a great gulping
breath in an effort to contain her agony.

'Are you...*Betsy*?' Gemma gasped.

'It's very warm in here,' Betsy mumbled and she
hurried outside where the cold breeze cooled the per-
spiration beading her brow.

'I didn't know you and *he*...I swear I didn't!' her
sister muttered uncomfortably. 'I'd never have given
you that photo if I'd had the least idea—'

'I don't want to talk about this,' Betsy interposed
flatly, mastering her tempestuous emotions.

'It's hard not to...I mean, you don't seem to have
much luck with men,' Gemma pointed out. 'Rory and
that thug, Joe...and *then*—'

'Rat of the century, Cristos Stephanides? Let's not
go there either,' Betsy advised curtly and, for once,
her sister was silenced.

On the way home to her bedsit, Betsy bought herself
a pregnancy test. That evening the packet containing
her purchase sat in solitary state on the table. It was
the last thing she looked at before she switched out
the light and the first thing she noticed in the morning.
She did not sleep well. Telling herself to act like a
grown-up instead of a scared teenager, Betsy did the
test. It came up positive and the shock was so great
she burst into floods of tears.

How on earth was she going to cope as an unmarried mother? She didn't earn enough to pay for full-time childcare. There was no way she could juggle a new baby and restore classic cars either. She would not be in a position to live on a shoestring and put in the long hours that any new business demanded. In short, her goose had been well and truly cooked and who had thrown her independent, perfectly free and happy life to the lions? Cristos Stephanides!

Why was it that the one time she had decided to take a risk on a guy she had been well and truly punished? It had taken Cristos little more than twenty-four hours to talk her into bed. She had been a very easy conquest. Shame made her squirm. At the time it had seemed so brave to throw away all caution and follow her feelings. Now she just felt plain stupid. She had acted like a slut, she thought painfully. Was it any wonder that Cristos had had no respect for her and the neck to offer her a place in his life as his mistress?

But what about all those fine promises he had made to her? About how he would be with her every step of the way if she fell pregnant? About how she could trust and depend on him…oh, yeah, and all the time he had been engaged to another woman! How could he have done that to her? From where had he got the nerve to approach her again? Had Cristos no sense of shame? Tears blinding her, she rocked back and forth on the side of her bed.

Why had she had to find Cristos so irresistibly attractive? Every time he'd smiled, she had carried on like a teenager. She had cooked for him and hand-washed his shirts. Without effort, he had turned her into a domestic slave. Poor Rory had been told that if they got married he would have to do his own washing and that it was about time he learned to cook so that he could take a turn. Had she made Cristos take a turn on the domestic front?

No, having fallen in love, she had been all sweetness and light. She had wanted everything to be perfect for him. Now she was going to have a baby, *his* baby. She imagined that that news would be one of the biggest shocks that Cristos had ever had. At their last meeting, he had been so blithely unconcerned by the possibility of consequences that he had not even bothered to ask her if she was all right. Cristos exuded the cool expectation and confidence of a male who had always led a charmed life. The kidnapping had been a major shock to his equilibrium. However, she thought it painfully typical of Cristos' charmed existence that when he was kidnapped he had been put on an idyllic island in luxury accommodation with good food and a willing bed partner thrown in.

On the other hand it seemed that his luck had ended there, Betsy conceded unhappily. Evidently her luck had been at its lowest ebb too. Cristos would not find it easy to handle her news. It would not be any easier for her to tell him. After all, how pleasant could it be to inform a guy who was engaged to someone else that you were carrying his baby? A baby he couldn't possibly want? A baby that would only be a source of annoyance and an embarrassment to him?

Betsy breathed in deep and scolded herself for getting so upset. After all, she could not afford to be oversensitive. Cristos would have to be told. She had to be sensible and consider the baby's needs and her own. Furthermore, it took two to make a baby, which meant that he was as much to blame as she was...

CHAPTER SIX

FEELING stiff and uncomfortable in the sober dark brown skirt suit she had dug out of the back of her wardrobe, Betsy sat down in the elegant waiting area on the executive floor of the Stephanides office block.

With an unsteady hand, she lifted an architectural digest adorned with a picture of the strikingly contemporary and comparatively new building. She opened it up, was confronted by a photo of Cristos smiling and hastily returned the magazine to the coffee-table.

'Miss Mitchell?' A svelte older woman approached her with a cordless phone. 'Mr Stephanides asked me to offer you his apologies. He's in an important meeting but he would like to speak to you.'

Bemused, Betsy accepted the proffered receiver.

'I'm so pleased you're here. We'll have lunch together,' Cristos murmured huskily and somewhere in the background she could hear the dulled drone of male voices talking.

Betsy tensed, for she had not viewed her visit as being in the light of a social occasion. 'But—'

'I'd love to chat but I can't. Listen, I've already arranged transport for you and Dolius will take you downstairs. I'll wrap up things here within the hour and join you.'

Before she could catch her breath, Cristos had terminated the call. She should have told him in advance that she was coming to see him or at least made an appointment, Betsy reflected uncomfortably. The bodyguard whom she had crossed swords with on the day of the kidnapping stepped out of the lift.

'Will you come this way, please?' Dolius enquired, his craggy features as expressionless as though he had never met her before.

For the first time in her life, Betsy travelled as a passenger in a luxurious limousine. But she could not relax enough to get anything out of the experience. Her nerves were as active as jumping beans. Where was she being taken? Some hotel? She could hardly announce that she was pregnant over lunch in a public restaurant. When Cristos arrived she would have to explain that she needed to speak to him in private.

Her every expectation was confounded when she was taken to an exclusive block of accommodation and ushered up to the penthouse. Assuming that the palatial apartment was where Cristos lived when he was over in London, Betsy paced the carpet in the magnificent drawing room. It was, however, a curiously impersonal room. It had neither photos nor books; indeed there was nothing on display that would have cast the smallest light on the nature, family connections or interests of the owner. At the other end of the apartment, the distant clatter of dishes and voices indicated that lunch was being prepared.

'Betsy…'

She whirled round.

Dark eyes flaming gold, Cristos stared across the room at her. 'So how do we celebrate this historic moment?' he drawled.

His business suit was a dark grey pinstripe tailored to an exquisite fit on his broad shoulders and long, powerful thighs. His slow, devastating smile slashed his darkly handsome features. For a shameful instant, her heart leapt inside her chest with excitement. A split second later, she remembered Petrina Rhodias and the pain of that humiliating recollection stiffened her backbone.

'What historic moment?' Betsy echoed, struggling to regain her concentration and say what had to be said. *'Celebrate?'*

'This apartment is yours. I bought it for you soon after we regained our freedom,' Cristos imparted, strolling forward. 'But if you don't like it, we'll find you somewhere more to your taste.'

It was only then that Betsy realised that Cristos had got completely the wrong idea about why she had come to see him. 'If you bought this apartment for me, you've made a really expensive mistake. I don't understand why you won't listen to what I say to you—'

'How can I?' Cristos demanded. 'I want you back. Why are you doing this to us? You look miserable—'

'Yes...' Betsy conceded tightly. 'You've got that right. But you've got everything else wrong. In fact we're talking at cross purposes. I wanted to see you today for one reason only—'

'Let's discuss it at our leisure over lunch,' Cristos cut in, smooth as silk.

'I don't feel sociable...look—' Betsy hesitated and then stabbed on '—I'm pregnant.'

Cristos went so still he might have been a statue. His expression did not alter but his superb bone structure tightened beneath his bronzed skin. The silence went on and on, nagging at her ragged nerves.

'Are you sure?' Cristos asked with pronounced clarity.

His dark eyes no longer flamed gold. His gaze had grown sombre. The care with which he spoke and the sudden definable edge of his Greek accent betrayed the level of the shock she had dealt him.

'Yes. I saw a doctor yesterday.' In the tense silence, Betsy dragged in a quivering breath. 'He confirmed what I already knew.'

His hard jaw line squared. 'And you chose my office as the ideal place to make such an announcement?'

A rueful little laugh fell from her lips. 'I don't know where you live when you're in London. Have you forgotten that? It really seems to say it all, doesn't it? Here I am, pregnant by a man whose address I don't even know!'

'I don't see the significance of my address.'

'I didn't think you would. You have the sensitivity of a concrete block.'

'Would you like a drink?' Cristos spoke as though she had not, his rich, dark drawl laced with excessive politeness.

Feeling cut off, Betsy reddened. 'Anything…'

'But not, of course, something alcoholic,' Cristos affixed with innate arrogance.

Rage shot through Betsy's slight frame like an adrenalin jag. Within ten seconds of learning that she was pregnant, Cristos was laying down the law with a galling air of superior authority. 'Know a lot…do you…about how to treat women in my condition?'

'Only what is common knowledge,' Cristos murmured with unimpeachable modesty.

'Well, let's hope you know more about the health issues of being pregnant than you knew about the risks of getting pregnant!' Betsy shot at him accusingly.

'So blame is to be apportioned.' Cristos raised an

infuriating winged dark brow. 'Is that what you call constructive?'

It was like a red rag to a bull. 'No, it's not constructive but it expresses how I feel and that is horribly bitter and angry!' Betsy admitted. 'When we were on Mos, I trusted you. You made loads of really impressive promises. You swore you would stand by me if anything went wrong—'

'Perhaps your unfortunate experiences with other men have misled you,' Cristos murmured flatly, pressing the bell on the wall.

'What's that supposed to mean?'

'You're not used to men you can rely on—'

'Don't you dare tell me that I can rely on you!' Betsy warned him, her incredulity at his sheer nerve unconcealed. 'Don't you *dare*!'

'Don't judge me without giving me a chance—'

'Don't throw Rory and one date with a kidnapper in my face!' Betsy traded fiercely. 'You do it one more time to me and I'll scream!'

'This is degenerating into a very unproductive confrontation.'

'After all, if you want to discuss my lack of judgement when it comes to men, please include yourself in that study,' Betsy slung back at him, refusing to back down. 'If you're honest, you will then see that you have caused me the most grief and the most damage. Being pregnant at this stage of my life will destroy all my future plans.'

Cristos said nothing. Her announcement had had a similar effect on him to watching a huge tidal wave wreak havoc while he stood powerless on the sidelines. Within seconds and with an immediacy that would have shaken her, for she had little faith in him, he had known what he must do and what would be the results. And the results even from a business and family point of view would be disastrous. The merger with the Rhodias clan would crash and burn at spectacular speed. The inevitable battle that would follow would be very bloody and very dirty. Share prices would fall, stockholders would get nervous, takeover bids would be launched. Job losses and restructuring would be inevitable. For the foreseeable future he would be working eighteen-hour days…

Tears stinging her eyes, Betsy spun away to stare blindly out the window. She was getting really emotional and she had tried so hard to stay calm. But her doctor had warned her about the often unsettling emotional effects of early pregnancy. Certainly she had never cried or shouted so much as she had in recent days. All she was doing, though, was making a bad situation worse. What was the point of hurling recriminations at Cristos? Where was the advantage in encouraging him to think she was a shrew? She was a grown woman and she had taken the same risk with him and should accept equal responsibility for the new life forming within her womb.

A light knock broke the silence and she spun back. An older man, who seemed to be an employee, was inclining his head to receive instructions from Cristos. Dully she watched the man open the drinks cabinet and proceed to pour brandy for Cristos and a soft drink that was presumably for her. She blinked, belatedly understanding the significance of the bell that Cristos had pressed. She mumbled thanks for the glass presented to her on a tray.

'Cristos…' she whispered shakily as the manservant withdrew. 'You just rang a bell and summoned another person to pour two drinks from a cabinet only ten feet away from you.'

His winged ebony brows pleated. 'What of it?'

'Oh…nothing,' she muttered.

His sublime lack of comprehension had penetrated. She went pink. He was accustomed to servants. Of course he was. He was not used to performing menial tasks on his own account. No wonder he had never seemed comfortable in the kitchen and had refused to eat there. No wonder he had gone into the dishwasher when she'd asked him to fetch her something out of the fridge. Domestically speaking, he was Stone Age man. When he had watched her ironing his shirt with apparent fascination and had commented about how much work it was, that had not been a back-handed way of thanking her but a sincere opinion of a task new to his experience.

Sipping at her drink, she watched him from below her lashes. Lean, strong face set, he looked as bleak as she felt. She could not bear to be responsible for that. For a moment she honestly thought her heart were breaking in two inside her. Certainly anything that had remained of her pride was swept away for ever in that instant. She still loved him and it seemed the final humiliation to know that right now he had to be deeply regretting ever laying eyes on her…wishing he hadn't noticed her that day in the airport car park.

His vibrantly handsome features grave, Cristos surveyed her. 'You're angry that you're pregnant and you're angry with me. I understand that. But I would like to know how you feel about this baby.'

Her vulnerable gaze widened and then veiled. It was like being asked to define the need for world peace in five seconds. How *did* she feel about the baby? She had not yet had time to consider the child she carried as a tiny person in its own right. But she did know that she felt guilty that she was not in a position to offer her baby more stable prospects and a father. She had a secret fear that she might turn out to be really hopeless in the parenting stakes. She also knew that she was genuinely afraid of the huge burden of responsibility that would fall on her shoulders. However, she was ashamed about all those feelings and could not bring herself to admit them to him.

'I am aware that this is a difficult time for you—' Cristos appeared to be picking his words with unusual care and she glanced up '—but decisions must be made and we need to be honest with each other.'

Betsy tensed. 'I don't want an abortion.'

'Is that what you thought I was asking?' His beautiful mouth quirked but his gaze was level. 'This is my child too. I was brought up to respect the ties of family beyond all others. This child will be my son or my daughter and the next generation in the Stephanides family. If you had wanted a termination, I would be trying to change your mind—'

'I don't think I can believe you when you say that,' Betsy muttered unhappily. 'What choice have you got?'

'There is always a choice. If I wanted nothing to do with this child, if I was prepared to walk away, I could make generous financial provision for you both. But I could not live with the option of never knowing my own flesh and blood,' Cristos confessed. 'My grandfather set me an example when my parents died.'

'How?' she whispered.

'When they died, Patras was about to embark on a fun-filled retirement and a second marriage with a much younger woman. I was eleven years old. For my benefit, Patras made sacrifices. He stayed at the helm of the Stephanides empire to conserve my inheritance. Even though he loved the woman, he gave her up because he knew that she wasn't stepmother material.'

Hurt tears prickled at the back of her nose. 'I really don't want to be your sacrifice, Cristos.'

'I'm not thinking about you...I'm thinking about our child,' Cristos pointed out drily. 'We're adults. We can sort ourselves out. This baby will only have us to depend on. I feel bound by my honour to offer our child a stable environment in which to live.'

'I don't drink or do drugs, so I don't believe that you need to speak as if I'm a totally unsuitable person to have the care of a child,' Betsy protested stiffly.

Cristos expelled his breath in an impatient hiss. 'You are determined to take offence. Can't you rise above your hostility and focus on the bigger picture? I didn't suggest that you would be an inadequate parent. But even you cannot deny that our child would benefit most from having two parents, who are married to each other.'

Her brow pleated in confusion. Her back was aching from the stress of standing rigid for so long. Surrendering to her discomfort, she sank down heavily on the sofa behind her. 'Run that by me again... married to each other?'

Brilliant dark eyes flashed gold over her. Cristos flung his arms wide in a volatile gesture of expressive frustration. 'Obviously we're going to have to get married!'

'Oh, no, we're not...go lay your sacrificial head on someone else's block!' Betsy advised, fighting to keep the lid on her absolute astonishment that he should even consider offering matrimony. 'I want to do the best I can for our baby as well, but wild horses wouldn't get me to the altar with a guy like you!'

'What do you mean…a guy like me?' Cristos demanded.

'You're engaged to another woman yet you've slept with me and you've asked me to be your mistress. With that evidence, I don't need to be bright to deduce that you would be the equivalent of the husband from hell!'

Outrage flamed through Cristos at that blunt response. 'I will be an excellent husband and father.'

Betsy tilted up her chin. 'But you won't be *my* husband.'

In the silence that spread like an oil slick waiting on a torch to ignite, the manservant crept in to announce that lunch was being served.

'I'm not hungry,' Betsy said thinly.

Cristos seared her with one glance. 'But possibly the baby is, so you can make an effort.'

In a room across the hall, a polished mahogany table had been laid with beautiful china. In any other mood, Betsy would have been impressed to death. However, she was still in too much shock from the revelation that Cristos was prepared to call off his engagement to do what had once been called, 'the decent thing' and give their child his name. Just as he had promised on the island, he was willing to support her through her pregnancy.

'You must not judge me on the basis of my relationship with Petrina,' Cristos drawled with supreme cool. 'Naturally you don't understand the bond that I have with her and it is not necessary that you should.

Some matters are private and not on the table for discussion—'

'Which is a very long-winded and patronising way of saying that you're the unfaithful type and not prepared to change,' Betsy filled in, her luscious pink mouth taking on a scornful curl.

Arrogant head high, lean, strong face hard, Cristos dealt her a steady appraisal that made her shift uneasily in her seat. 'I have asked you to marry me. Whatever else I may deserve, I don't believe that is an excuse for you to insult me.'

Mortified colour burned Betsy's skin. She felt like a child being rebuked for rudeness.

'I don't make idle promises. To the best of my ability, I would try to make our marriage work—'

'For the baby's sake,' she slotted in half under her breath, her throat aching.

'For *all* our sakes,' Cristos contradicted.

Mulling that over, striving to at least respect his good intentions even if she did not wish to be the charitable target of them, Betsy ate her fresh-fruit starter. 'Do you like children?'

'Very much…I may not have surviving siblings but I do have many cousins. Most of them have offspring.'

She had not been prepared for that wholehearted response. He liked kids. Then he would have expected to have children with Petrina Rhodias. Did he love Petrina? Love and fidelity did not always go hand in hand. Not everyone placed the same importance on physical fidelity. But Betsy placed huge importance on it. How could Petrina bear to know that Cristos slept with other women? Didn't she mind? Or didn't she know? Did Petrina love Cristos so much that she was willing to share him? Her thoughts revolving in a mad, frantic whirl, Betsy drew in a slow steadying breath.

'Talk about what you're thinking…raise your concerns.' Cristos leant back in his armchair, his glass of wine cradled in one lean brown hand. His black hair gleaming in the light from the window, bold bronzed features intent, he looked incredibly handsome. He also looked every inch what he was, she conceded heavily. A Greek tycoon from a privileged world, an intelligent, cultured and sophisticated male. Yet in her opinion he was letting an old-fashioned sense of honour come between him and common sense.

'It wouldn't work,' she told him tightly. 'You and I. We're chalk and cheese—'

'That's stimulating—'

'We fight all the time!'

His dark eyes glittered, his wide, sensual mouth curving to reveal a glimmer of even white teeth. 'And then we forget our differences in bed. We have passion. Respect it, *pethi mou.*'

'It would never be enough for either of us,' Betsy told him flatly, pain infiltrating her.

Would he ever recognise how lucky he was that she was turning him down? He drove her crazy but she loved him. It would be so easy to be selfish. And she was convinced that it would be selfish to let him marry her. If he cared for anyone, she was convinced it would be Petrina with whom he had so much more in common. Betsy was sure that he would be willing to help her financially. Just a little practical help would enable her to remain pretty much independent and he would be free to go on with his life and marry his beautiful heiress.

After all, Petrina was the innocent party, Betsy conceded guiltily. When she remembered the unhappiness that Rory's infidelity with Gemma had caused her personally, she knew that she could not do the same thing to another woman. Yes, maybe it would cost Cristos to have to live with the awareness that he had a child he did not see. But no compromise was perfect.

'You're not being honest with me.' Glittering dark eyes raked her pale, taut, guilty face with condemnation. 'You're in love with your sister's boyfriend and their relationship is on the rocks. I think you're hoping to get him back—'

'That's absolute nonsense!' Betsy was seriously affronted that he could deem her capable of such calculating and low behaviour.

'I doubt very much that he will want you with my child inside you and with me *very* much on the scene,' Cristos forecast with burning derision.

Thrusting back her chair in a temper, Betsy threw herself upright. Without warning she was assailed by a powerful wave of giddiness and nausea. Swaying, she had time only to utter a faint moan of protest before she folded down into the claustrophobic darkness of a faint.

'Lie still…' Cristos urged when she began to regain consciousness.

For once she did not argue. She still felt sick. It was bad enough having fainted but there were even more embarrassing scenarios. She concentrated on controlling the nausea and kept her eyes closed. Cristos was talking to someone in low, urgent tones. She heard him replace a phone and she breathed in slowly to try and ward off the lingering sensation of being lightheaded.

He curved his arms round her very gently and lifted

her. Unexpectedly her eyes filled with tears and she kept her eyes tight shut, willing them back. But when he settled her down on a bed, she began sitting up. 'I'm OK—'

'You're *not*,' Cristos delivered. 'It's my fault you collapsed. I upset you. I shouldn't have been arguing with you—'

'Pregnant women get dizzy…goes with the territory,' she muttered chokily, feeling horribly sorry for herself.

Cristos looked unconvinced. 'At least take it easy until the doctor arrives.'

'Why did you call a doctor?' she groaned. 'There was no need for that.'

In due course a suave older man from the private sector arrived. He was cheerful and brisk but he told her that she was exhausted and needed to take more care of herself. Cristos made no attempt to conceal his concern. She was almost willing to admit that she was so tired she could hardly lift her head from the pillow. 'I'll have a nap,' she finally conceded.

Cristos watched her from the foot of the bed, his spiky black lashes low over his incisive dark golden eyes. 'I should warn you that I haven't changed my mind, *pethi mou*. I still intend to marry you. I want the right to look after you and my proper place in my child's life. You will never convince me that there is a better option.'

'Right now I'm too sleepy to try.' Her softened green eyes lingered on his heartbreakingly handsome features and then, with a self-conscious flush, she turned her head away. 'I'm sorry I didn't believe you'd stick to the promises you made,' she muttered unevenly. 'I know you think you've come up with the best solution and I respect that. But women don't have to marry these days just to raise a child.'

'A Stephanides woman does.'

He was immoveable as a rock and she was amused. She drifted off into a heavy sleep with a faint curve to her weary mouth and slept for several hours. She had wakened and sat up, feeling very much refreshed by her nap when Cristos came in and extended a phone to her. 'For you…your parents want to speak to you…'

'My parents?' she mouthed in disbelief back at him, but the door was already closing on his exit.

'Betsy…' Corinne Mitchell said chirpily. 'Your father and I just couldn't wait a minute longer to phone you. While you were resting, Cristos called us and introduced himself—'

'Cristos did…*what*?' Betsy prompted weakly.

'He's really worried about you doing too much…and he's dying to meet us—'

Betsy had gone rigid. 'Is he really?'

'I have to confess that we are *very* taken with him. I know he's so handsome and he has lovely manners when you talk to him. And he seems to be terribly well off. I know you think money shouldn't be important but I like a man to be a good provider—'

'Cristos is insisting that he will pay for the wedding,' Betsy's father chimed in, evidently on an extension line.

'Yes, he's so generous and considerate,' Corinne Mitchell enthused. 'Mind you, I would normally be a little upset about your being pregnant—'

'Cristos told you?' Betsy yelped in appalled embarrassment.

'But you'll be married soon enough and at least he's

not expecting you to be happy about being an unmarried mother like Rory does Gemma.'

'No, I must say you can't fault Cristos there,' her father pronounced with hearty approval. 'He can't wait to put a ring on your finger.'

'Where did you get the idea that Cristos and I might be getting married?' Betsy asked rather shrilly.

'When he suggested we draw up a full list of the guests we want to invite,' Corinne explained with palpable excitement. 'He said we could ask as many people as we like. Don't tease me, Betsy. We're just over the moon for you. I've already phoned half of our relatives to tell them our good news. Maybe a big wedding will put Rory in the notion.'

'It's a relief that your sister has made up with Rory,' her father commented. 'You'll be able to have Gemma as a bridesmaid—'

'No, she won't!' his wife interrupted in dismay. 'Gemma wants to be a bride too much to act as Betsy's bridesmaid. Much better just to have little Sophie.'

Those frank opinions having been exchanged, Betsy managed to finish the call by promising to ring back later. She was filled with shaken disbelief at the trap that Cristos had sprung on her without conscience. How could he have sunk so low? She could not credit that he had chosen to use her unsuspecting parents to put pressure on her. Her poor mother had started telling people that her eldest daughter was getting hitched, and if no wedding came off Corinne Mitchell would be devastated and humiliated.

Betsy found Cristos in the drawing room, talking on a phone in Greek. Brilliant dark eyes met hers with stubborn cool. He set the phone aside.

'How *could* you?' she pressed.

'Some day you'll look back on this and appreciate that I had your best interests at heart,' Cristos asserted smoothly.

'All you had at heart was your usual determination to do exactly what you want to do because you always think you're right!'

'You could have a point.' Cristos seemed determined to maintain a low profile in the aggression stakes.

'How am I supposed to tell my mum and dad that I don't want to marry you? Especially now they know I'm expecting a baby!' Betsy demanded in reproachful appeal.

'I can see you might have a problem.'

'I just can't believe you've done this to me…going calling my family and announcing that we're getting married when you know I've said no. You had no right to do that and involve them when they have no idea what's going on between us. I feel like I'm being blackmailed.'

'How do you feel otherwise?' Cristos enquired as if such accusations as she had made came his way every day and were unworthy of comment.

'Well, I feel just wonderful, Cristos!' Betsy slammed back at him. 'You're set on wrecking both our lives by forcing me in a direction I don't want to go. You can't do this to Petrina…it's so cruel—'

His hard bone structure clenched. 'Allow me to worry about Petrina—'

'I can't bear to hurt another woman the way I was hurt by Rory!' Betsy confided in distress.

His golden eyes shimmered, his lean, powerful face taut. 'The baby must have first claim on your loyalty and mine.'

Her slight shoulders slumped. He reached out to close his hands over hers and draw her close. She refused to look at him because she knew she could not trust herself.

'Stop tying yourself up in knots, *pethi mou*,' Cristos urged, the low-pitched timbre of his deep voice already achingly familiar to her. 'Why upset yourself over what can't be altered? I intervened with your parents because I want us to marry quickly. I see no reason why we should publicise the fact that we're getting married now because you're carrying our first child.'

Her fingers trembled in his. He knew how to press the right emotional buttons. Our *first* child. He was inviting her to look into a future that contained a real marriage in which other children would be welcomed as well. Her throat thickened and it was an effort for her to swallow. She really, really wanted to marry him.

'But wouldn't you feel trapped?' she prompted half under her breath. 'Wouldn't you resent me?'

Cristos closed one hand into the thick tumbling fall of her Titian hair to tug her head up. Stunning dark golden eyes met her troubled gaze in a direct onslaught. 'Never. I want you. I want our child as well.'

She braced a hand against his shoulder, let her fingers splay there in the shy but feeling touch of a woman longing to make physical contact. 'You'd have to be faithful...no excuses, no slips. I'd help you...I'd watch you like a hawk,' she warned him. 'You won't get away with anything, not even a flirtation if you marry me. Could you live like that?'

'Is there a choice?' Cristos dared.

Her green eyes fired up. 'No, and one strike and you're out too.'

'But you'll marry me.'

Today if you can fix it, she almost said. Fortunately she was too worked up to find her voice and it was only possible to nod, and she tried to nod with cool as if it were no big deal.

CHAPTER SEVEN

IT WAS Betsy's wedding day and she had never been happier.

A diamond tiara sparkling on her head, she studied her reflection in the cheval-mirror. Having fallen in love with the emerald silk bustier on sight, she had teamed it with a flowing ivory skirt that enhanced the elegance of her tall, slender figure. As an outfit, it just screamed Cristos at her. Green was his favourite colour. He liked her hair loose too, and her vibrant coppery-red mane hung as waterfall-straight down her narrow back as a sheet of silk.

From the minute she had agreed to marry Cristos two weeks earlier, she had entered another world. But undoubtedly the toughest challenge, she reflected ruefully, had been barely seeing Cristos since then. He had had to return to Greece and after that there had been a business trip to New York. On the single occasion when they had been together, there had been a crowd present. Two members of his staff had dealt most efficiently with the wedding arrangements while still allowing Corinne Mitchell to feel that her input was highly important. In truth, though, Betsy's parents stood in total awe of their future son-in-law and had deemed the organisation of a social event for hundreds of wealthy important people to be way out of their league.

At Cristos' instigation, Betsy had given up her job and moved into the apartment, and for convenience her parents had been staying there with her. She had been amazed not just at the cloak of secrecy that Cristos seemed determined to cast over their big day but also at the elaborate security plans that he had insisted were necessary. He had suggested that the press might be tempted to make what he had termed, 'a nuisance of themselves' and that, in that event, she and her family would be safe from annoyance at the apartment. Betsy still could not credit that newspaper reporters would be even remotely interested in her.

'How do you think you'll fit in with Cristos' rich friends?' Gemma remarked. 'Do you think they'll like you?'

Betsy turned her dreamy gaze slowly from the mirror. 'I hope so. People are people whether they're rich or not—'

'Well, his grandfather's obviously not too pleased about the switch in brides. I notice he hasn't made any special effort to welcome you into the family.'

Betsy was becoming tense. 'Why should he have done? He's eighty-three years old and I expect he's quite happy to wait until he meets me today. Let's not make assumptions—'

'I just suspect that your wonderful new life in Greece may not be a bed of roses. Cristos seems to go abroad a lot on business too.' Gemma sighed, somehow contriving to vocalise Betsy's every secret concern about her future as a wife. 'With a hunk as good-looking as Cristos, that'll be a real worry for you.'

'Why should it be a worry for me?' Betsy demanded for, while she ignored gibes angled at her, she could not bear to hear a word spoken against Cristos.

'Oh, come on...' Her sister vented a suggestive

laugh. 'Loads of girls would do *anything* to pull a guy like Cristos. He'll have to be a saint not to take advantage of the offers he must get. You're pregnant too and, let's face it, there's nothing sexy about a big tummy!'

If Corinne Mitchell had not popped her head round the door at that instant to tell Gemma that the bridesmaids' car had arrived, Betsy honestly thought she might have screamed. She looked down at her still-flat mid-section and grimaced. Would Cristos find her unattractive when she lost her waist? If he did, he was hardly likely to admit the fact.

The phone buzzed and she swept it up. 'Did she bitch at you?' Cristos asked, smooth as silk.

'I'm not answering that.' Involuntarily, however, a reluctant grin began chasing the strain from Betsy's raspberry-tinted mouth.

'I warned you not to have your sister as a bridesmaid,' Cristos reminded her softly. 'I only had to spend five minutes in the same room to see that she's a jealous little cat who can't stand not to be the centre of attention.'

'Don't be unkind,' Betsy scolded him. 'Gemma is just going through a rough patch right now.'

'Before I forget,' Cristos murmured then with studied casualness, 'there's a very large press contingent encamped outside the church. Ignore them. Dolius has arranged extra security cover—'

'But why should they be that interested in our wedding?' Betsy frowned. 'Are you so important?'

'No, I suspect they've heard a rumour about how very, very beautiful my bride is,' Cristos said, deadpan.

Thirty minutes later, climbing into the wedding car

with her proud father in tow, Betsy was still smiling. Although Cristos had warned her that the press was besieging the church, Betsy was still aghast at the sheer number of people waving cameras and shouting. Crash barriers were being employed and security men were standing shoulder to shoulder.

'Good grief...the television cameras will be along next!' her astonished father quipped.

Flash bulbs went off. Betsy kept her head down while Dolius strong-armed a passage into the church porch where he slammed shut the heavy wooden door. The calm and peace enfolded her, soothing her nerves. She was about to marry the man she loved, she reminded herself: it was going to be a fantastic day.

At the altar, formally garbed in a superb light grey suit, Cristos looked so spectacular, her tummy flipped. During the ceremony, he made his responses in a clear, crisp voice. She stumbled badly over his middle name, which she had never heard until that moment, and blushed in severe embarrassment. He was still smiling when he put the ring on her finger. They went to sign the register and she whispered, 'How on earth do you pronounce that name?'

'Xanthos.'

'I needed coaching for that one.'

As they walked down the aisle there was standing room only in the packed church. Cristos had a light arm curved to her spine. Her head was high and her eyes shone because he leant close to tell her how fantastic she looked.

'Now...you are a Stephanides and you must learn how to deal with the paparazzi,' Cristos informed her in calm continuance.

'How?'

'You ignore them,' he instructed her. 'No matter what you are asked, you don't listen, you don't answer, you don't look at them and you don't ever let your face reveal any response.'

'In other words, I am to stick my nose in the air and act like the press are absolutely beneath my notice,' Betsy paraphrased with bubbling amusement because she was in such a happy mood she could not be serious.

His arm tightened round her. 'The press can be cruel. Be warned, *yineka mou*.'

They walked out onto the church steps. The cameras went into a frenzy of flashing and clicking and requests to look this way and that flew from all directions and in more than one language. At the same time questions were being shouted. Cristos was urging her towards the limo when a raucous voice from quite close at hand yelled clear as a bell, 'Betsy…when's the baby due?'

Almost imperceptibly, she flinched but kept moving.

'Being kidnapped with Cristos has really paid off for you!' A dirty laugh punctuated that statement. 'Care to comment?' someone else bawled.

'Are you sure the kid wasn't fathered by your lover, Joe Tyler?'

When she fell abruptly still, white with shock and horror, Cristos let go of her and launched himself at the man who had hurled that final insulting question. Dolius practically lifted Betsy to get her into the shelter of the limo and then went back in haste to bodily retrieve Cristos from the fistfight breaking out. Hands braced to steady herself on the seat, her face stiff with humiliation, Betsy was trembling in disbelief.

Her pregnancy was no longer a secret known only to her family. The press knew she was expecting Cristos' baby. How could that have happened? The paparazzi also knew about the kidnapping and about Joe as well. She felt stripped naked and exposed. Her wedding day was absolutely destroyed.

Cristos swung into the car with athletic ease. He met her anguished gaze and shrugged. 'I knew they were on to us before I arrived at the church. I didn't want it to spoil your day—'

'It's a nightmare...' Betsy mumbled.

Temper back under control, Cristos flexed bruised knuckles with very male cool and acceptance. 'If it's any consolation, I hit the bastard who made that filthy comment.'

It wasn't. The guy who had told her how *not* to behave around journalists had just broken all his own rules because of something that had been said to her. She had become a source of embarrassment to Cristos. The whole world was now acquainted with the lowering fact that he had made a shotgun marriage. Even worse, nasty rumours about her relationship with the late Joe Tyler were doing the rounds. And, to top it all, Betsy reflected in positive anguish, absolutely everybody would be thinking what a slut she had to be to have gone to bed with Cristos when she hardly knew him!

'How did all the stuff about the kidnapping come out?' she pressed.

'It most probably came from more than one source. We did what we could to keep it quiet but perhaps too many people knew too much for it to remain buried,' Cristos breathed in a tone of regret.

Betsy could not really see why the kidnapping had

had to be hushed up to such an extent. She was a great deal more concerned by the much more personal nature of the revelations that had been thrown in her face in front of an audience. 'But who told them I was pregnant…who told them I'd ever even been out with Joe Tyler?' she gasped. 'I'd swear nobody at work knew about that one date!'

'I suspect that only a woman would time the revelations in the hope of wrecking our wedding day. No doubt tomorrow's papers will educate us as to the source of the leaks.' Cristos dealt her a bracing appraisal. 'Today, however, we have a wedding to celebrate and we must put this unpleasantness back out of our minds again.'

'But all your friends and family know that I'm pregnant now!' Betsy wailed.

'So we're fertile…' Cristos shrugged a broad shoulder with a magnificent disregard for her mortification. 'People love to gossip. Our guests will revel in all this controversy. Most weddings are rather boring.'

'Any day of the week, I'd choose to be bored rather than humiliated!'

'How does having my baby inside you humiliate you?' Cristos enquired, pulling her up against him and without warning splaying a bold hand across her stomach, lean brown fingers striking warmth and intimacy through the fabric that separated him from her skin.

Betsy found herself backtracking. 'I didn't mean it precisely that way. But I think it's really embarrassing that people should know that I slept with you so soon after meeting you…they'll all think I'm a slut,' she pointed out in a stifled undertone.

Cristos flipped her round and gave her a wholly unrepentant grin that radiated his natural charisma.

That grin made her want to hit him but it also sent her heart racing in a dual response that was becoming all too familiar to her in his radius.

'I'll take out full-page ads in all the major newspapers announcing that you were a virgin when we first shared a bed,' Cristos suggested levelly. 'Would that make you feel better?'

Thrusting herself free of him, Betsy studied him aghast. 'You're not serious?'

Glittering dark eyes gazed steadily back at her. 'I'm rather proud of the fact I was your first lover...I'd need very little encouragement to go public with the news. If you truly feel *so* humiliated—'

Betsy was pink to the roots of her hair. 'I don't feel *that* humiliated...you don't tell people stuff like that!'

Cristos closed an assured hand over hers, flung back his darkly handsome head and laughed with rich enjoyment.

Betsy launched herself back up against him and looked at him with a combination of chagrin, relief and grudging respect. 'You were teasing me!' she gasped, mortified that he had succeeded in fooling her.

Cristos folded an arm back round her and suddenly she twisted round and pressed into him to wind her arms tight round his neck. The feel of his lean, muscular body and the wonderfully familiar scent of his skin made her weak with longing. 'Sorry, I've been acting the diva,' she muttered guiltily. 'You're right...nothing should be allowed to cloud our day.'

In response, hard fingers tipped up her face. He drove her soft lips apart in a sensually savage kiss that brought her body alive with almost painful enthusiasm. 'I'm burning for you, *pethi mou*,' he growled with roughened urgency.

They had arrived at the hotel where the reception was to be held. The passenger door opened. Dolius' craggy face split into a smile at finding the bridal couple in each other's arms and then went poker-straight again.

Betsy had never met so many people in her entire life as she met at the wedding reception. Her head whirled with names and snatches of conversation. She was seated with Cristos before it dawned on her that she had yet to meet her bridegroom's closest relative, Patras Stephanides.

'Where's your grandfather?' Betsy asked in an urgent whisper. 'Didn't he want to sit at this table?'

'It may have passed your notice but my grandfather is not among our guests,' Cristos said stonily.

Betsy flushed. 'He's not here…why? Is he ill?'

'He chose not to attend.'

'For goodness' sake, why didn't you tell me?' Betsy whispered back in dismay. 'What an awful thing to do to you when you're so close! I'm so sorry—'

'It was my grandfather's right to choose not to be here. I won't have him criticised for it.' Grim dark eyes reproved her. 'His decision does not lessen my respect for him in any way.'

Betsy had lost colour. She tried not to feel hurt because she knew that she had touched a raw wound. Cristos was very attached to the older man. Naturally he was feeling the sting of his grandfather's decision to absent himself from so important a milestone in his grandson's life. At the same time Betsy could only feel as though she had been tried and found wanting. In opting out of their wedding, Patras Stephanides was expressing his uncompromising disapproval of the woman whom Cristos had decided to marry. Her heart sank because his grandfather's refusal to accept her was anything but a promising start to their marriage.

Later, after they had eaten and done a lot of socialising, which made any personal conversation impossible, Cristos drew her onto the dance floor. 'Stop brooding about Patras,' he instructed, demonstrating a dismaying ability to read her thoughts. 'He's as set in his ways as most men of his age and, in time, he'll come round.'

'Was he terribly fond of Petrina?' Betsy asked in a rush.

Cristos released his breath in a slow, measured hiss. 'It's not that simple. An engagement is a serious commitment in Greece. Having given my word that I would marry Petrina, I then asked to be released from it. Patras was devastated. The Rhodias family are outraged and Patras believes that I have dishonoured him.'

'And I bet he's blaming me for it.' Betsy sighed into his jacket, feeling more responsible than ever.

'There *was* no easy solution to our predicament,' Cristos murmured wryly, lean, strong face reflective. 'We have to be realistic. When you injure other people, there is always a price to pay.'

'But I don't want you to have to pay a price...' Betsy confided, disturbed that he had yet to make even the smallest reference to his own feelings regarding his broken engagement.

But then what on earth would be the point of Cristos confessing that he still cared about Petrina? It would change nothing and only make Betsy feel like an albatross round his neck. Having married her for the sake of their child, Cristos was the sort of guy who would make the best of their marriage. In fact he had already begun to act like a husband. He had tried to protect her from the hurtful intrusion of the press into their private lives. In a similar vein, he had not rushed to inform her that his grandfather was boycotting their wedding because he had known that that news would only upset her.

'I hope that a year from now you'll be able to look back and think that all this was worth it,' Betsy whispered earnestly.

'A year from now I'll be a father…I have no regrets now and I will have none then.' His beautifully shaped mouth quirked. 'Don't look for problems that aren't there.'

It was an excellent piece of advice but hard to follow. If he had loved her, she would have felt much stronger. It took two to make a baby, she thought unhappily. He had kept his promises to her because he was standing by her. For her sake, he had ended his engagement and as a result he was now estranged from his grandfather. He seemed to be the only one of them paying that price he had mentioned. After all, she loved Cristos and could hardly look on becoming his wife as being in any way a punishment.

Early evening, Cristos told her that they would soon have to leave. She went off to get changed in the hotel room set aside for that purpose and wondered where they were going on their honeymoon. Garbed in a funky pale blue tweed jacket teamed with a matching short skirt that was hemmed with a fringe, she was heading back towards the stairs when Rory accosted her.

'Can I have a word?' her former boyfriend asked earnestly.

'I've barely had a chance even to speak to you to-

day.' Forced to move out of the path of a chambermaid
and her trolley, Betsy backed round the corner and
then shifted across into the more private seating area
there.

'If you had taken the chance, Gemma would have
thrown a fit.' Rory sighed. 'But I'm coming to the
conclusion that that may be my fault. I haven't been
fair to Gemma or you. The more she made it plain
that she expected me to marry her, the more I dug my
heels in. Now I'm going to make up for it…'

Betsy was hanging on his every word, a big smile
building on her face.

'I've bought a ring,' he confided.

'Make sure you set the scene right…dinner out,
Mum babysitting Sophie,' Betsy warned him chokily,
her eyes overbright with happy tears. 'Gemma likes
everything perfect. Don't just bung the ring at her and
act like her acceptance is a foregone conclusion.'

'I've learned since I did that to you,' Rory confided
with gentle irony.

She flung her arms round him and sniffed and
laughed almost simultaneously. 'Just promise me one
thing…'

'What?' Smiling down at her, he closed his arms
round her and gave her a hug.

'Tell her that you care far more about her than you
ever did about me,' she urged, wiping at her damp
eyes with her fingers as she fell back from him again.
'I'd better get back downstairs…'

Rory only a step behind her, she walked round the
corner and cannoned straight into Cristos. All three of
them stopped dead. There was one of those horrid
awkward silences.

Inclining his head with perfect civility to Rory, Cristos murmured silkily to his bride, 'Are you ready?'

Their departure was swift rather than lingering. Within seconds of getting into the car, Betsy was smothering a yawn. It had been an incredibly exhausting day. 'I'm so tired,' she muttered apologetically.

'Then close your eyes and sleep…' Cristos said it as if it was the most reasonable thing in the world.

'Where are we going?'

'We're spending the night at my country house. Tomorrow, we'll fly to Greece.'

'It was a beautiful wedding,' she told him drowsily.

'Was it?'

Something in his tone made her tense. 'Are you teasing me again?'

'Yes…forgive my cruel sense of humour.' Lounging back into his corner of the limousine, Cristos tugged her back against him, encouraging her into a more relaxed and comfortable position. Kicking off her shoes, she curled up against him with a grateful sigh and that was the last thing she remembered for a long time.

When she opened her eyes again, she was in a beautiful bedroom furnished with timeless antiques and lit with gracious lamps. According to her watch, it was almost eleven at night and Betsy groaned in dismay. It certainly promised to be a wedding night to remember. Cristos had to be really fed up with her for sleeping for so long! Catching a glimpse of her tousled and crumpled reflection in the dresser mirror, she winced in even greater consternation. Her cases were sitting just inside the door.

Forty minutes later, breathless from the speed with which she had showered, reapplied a little make-up and donned her slinky midnight-blue silk nightdress, Betsy descended the sweeping staircase.

She found Cristos in the library. Jacket and tie discarded, white silk shirt open at his strong brown throat, he was staring down into the fire, a brandy goblet curled in one hand.

Her attention welded to his classic bronze profile, she hovered on the threshold. 'Cristos…'

He straightened, brooding dark golden eyes narrowing. 'What are you doing out of bed?'

It was not quite the welcome Betsy had been hoping for. 'It's our wedding night…'

'*Theos mou*…is that an invitation?' Cristos drawled in apparent wonderment, his intent gaze dropping from her softly parted lips down to the pouting thrust of breasts defined by the silky material of her nightdress.

'I suppose it is…' Betsy dragged in a quick shallow breath to steady herself. She felt very self-conscious. Her body was already reacting with enthusiastic awareness to his appraisal. The rosy crests of her nipples stirred behind the lace bodice, the swollen tips tender. Her heart was thumping an upscale beat. The atmosphere had grown thick and heavy.

'A duty screw…?' Cristos lifted an ebony brow, his lean, darkly handsome features stamped with derision. 'Is that what you're offering me?'

Her mouth fell open. 'A…what kind of a thing is that to say to me?'

'That if you're only offering me your body because I married you today, I can get by without it.' Cristos drained his brandy and set down the empty glass with a decisive snap. 'I'm not that desperate.'

Betsy stared back at him in shaken disbelief. 'Are

you drunk? Is that why you're speaking to me like this?'

'I saw you weeping over Rory at our wedding. All that chummy hugging and pawing was a rather nauseating turn-off.'

Her troubled brow began to clear as she realised that he had misinterpreted what he had seen. 'I wasn't exactly weeping over him—'

Hard dark eyes rested on her. 'You *were*—'

'But not in the way you seem to mean. At the minute, a sad story could make me cry buckets. If my emotions are stirred at all, my eyes start flooding with tears. It's embarrassing but according to the doctor it's just my hormones.' While noting that Cristos was looking deeply unimpressed, Betsy was eager to explain. 'Rory was telling me that he's about to ask Gemma to marry him—'

Cristos vented a roughened laugh. 'Which is why the pair of you were tucked into a hidden dark corner in each other's arms, was it? Next you'll be telling me you were crying with happiness!'

'Why didn't you tackle me about this earlier?' Betsy prompted worriedly. 'Why did you pretend everything was OK?'

'Let me see…' Cristos murmured flatly. 'How many reasons would you like? Five hundred wedding guests? The fact that you're carrying my baby and shouldn't be subjected to stressful scenes? Or the simple reality that you told me you loved Rory on Mos? It's not very fair to castigate you for it now, is it?'

While he'd spoken, Betsy's colour had fluctuated, and by the time he made that last statement she was embarrassed enough to instinctively turn away. What an idiot she had been ever to claim that she loved

Rory! Words employed to conserve her pride had come back to haunt her. She saw that she had no choice but to explain herself and with as much frankness as possible.

'That stuff about me loving Rory,' Betsy confided, cheeks hot, green eyes only contriving to meet his for an instant. 'It was a total fabrication. I just didn't want you getting the idea that I might be getting too keen on you, so I told what I saw as a harmless fib at the time.'

'A total fabrication...' Cristos repeated rather thickly, brilliant dark-as-midnight eyes locked to her guilty face.

'Yes...maybe it sounds a bit strange to you but you're a guy...at the time it seemed a good idea to lie,' Betsy completed awkwardly.

'I don't believe you,' Cristos asserted without the smallest hesitation.

Betsy winced, her smooth brow furrowing. She was very aware that she was not telling him the whole truth. On the other hand, she was highly reluctant to confide that at any stage of her relationship with Cristos she had genuinely believed that she was still in love with Rory. 'All right...I'll tell you the truth—'

'Wasn't that what I got a minute ago?' Cristos asked with dangerous quietness.

'It was a harmless, slightly doctored version,' Betsy muttered, horribly aware that, for someone stuck in a literal hot seat, she was not doing very well. 'The truth is that I remained very fond of Rory for quite a while after he and I broke up because I didn't get close to anyone else.'

The silence stretched.

'Is that it?' Cristos queried.

Betsy nodded jerkily, studying him with desperate intensity in an effort to read his thoughts. Right now the last thing their marriage required was his conviction that she was madly in love with another man.

'I thought there might be a version three in the pipeline…' Infuriatingly, Cristos elevated a questioning brow. 'No?'

Feeling like a child caught out in a shameful act, Betsy compressed her lips. 'No.'

'So why did you come looking for me?'

Her face flamed.

'I'm only teasing…' But there was no lightening flare of gold in his stunning gaze, no amused curve to the sculpted line of his beautifully shaped mouth. He could not even summon up a smile at the sure knowledge that he was married to a woman who lied so badly she embarrassed him.

'You do believe me, don't you? About Rory, I mean,' Betsy checked anxiously. 'It's so important that you do…I really want our marriage to work.'

His incisive gaze veiled. 'I believe you.'

Betsy tensed when it finally dawned on her that she was practically begging him to come upstairs and make love to her! Mortified by that conviction, she walked to the door, a tall, slender figure with a mane of copper hair that was a vibrant splash of colour against her pale skin and the dark blue of her nightdress. 'Goodnight, then,' she told him rather stiffly.

On the way up the stairs, she was thinking fast and furiously. This was the same guy who had hardly been able to keep his hands off her on the island. Why was he so uninterested? Did pregnancy make her seem less attractive to him? She might not have the big tummy yet but was he already looking at her and mentally endowing her with an imaginary one? Or was it possible that he mistakenly believed that sexual intimacy might endanger her pregnancy? Who knew what strange old-fashioned ideas he might be harbouring?

Shedding her nightdress, because there was not the smallest sign that Cristos had ever had any intention of even sharing the same room as her, she got into bed. She was reaching out to switch off the lights when her bridegroom entered. Cristos sent her a winging golden glance, kicked the door shut with an air of purpose and began to undress. Her hand fell back nerveless from the light.

'I need a shower…give me five minutes, *pethi mou*.'

He stripped where he stood. Out of the corner of her vision, she was maddeningly conscious of him. She listened to the shower running and wondered what had kept him from her earlier. Would she ever understand Cristos Stephanides? Would she ever learn to penetrate that tough facade that could keep her as much in the dark as a stone wall?

When Cristos returned to the bedroom, crystalline drops of water were still shimmering on the curling dark hair that accentuated his powerful pectoral muscles. 'You stayed awake for me…' he murmured lazily.

And that fast the atmosphere switched to electrifying. Her tummy tensed and flipped. Meeting his shimmering golden eyes, she was suddenly extraordinarily short of breath. 'I thought you weren't even going to sleep here,' she confided, relief making her chatter.

'Sleep is the last thing on my mind, *yineka mou*.' With a rueful laugh that sent a sizzle of awareness travelling down her backbone, Cristos flicked back the sheet and lounged beside her.

His first kiss sent fire slivering through her tautness and made her melt from the outside in. Her hands coiled tight in on themselves. The silky touch of his tongue flicked the roof of her mouth. She gasped and he shifted against her, acquainting her with the bold potency of his arousal.

He let his lips travel hungrily down to the delicate skin of her throat and she rubbed against him with helpless encouragement, reacting to the tormenting pressure of his mouth in certain places. He toyed with her urgently sensitive nipples, suckled the straining pink buds until she was clutching at him and crying out helpless in the grip of her own excitement.

'It's time you stopped being so shy and learned how to please me...' Cristos breathed thickly, guiding her down to his hard male heat with an unconcealed urgency that had the most wickedly erotic effect on her.

Touching him, she trembled. The very scent of his bronzed skin was an aphrodisiac to her. She was eager to please and even keener to learn because his response to her was hot and sensual and undeniable.

Tangling long fingers in her Titian hair, he drew her back up to him. 'Fast learner...' he acknowledged raggedly, claiming her reddened mouth in a fierce, drugging kiss. 'We've been apart too long. I remember the island in my dreams...I could devour you.'

His skilful fingers found the liquid heat pulsing between her thighs. She squirmed, her hips rising in helpless supplication. Her body was tight and aching with readiness and she moaned out loud, controlled by the bittersweet intensity of the pleasure. 'Cristos...'

His smouldering golden gaze connected with the

plea in her passion-glazed eyes. In one lithe, powerful movement, he came over her and into her. In the throbbing agony of need, she was gripped by the headiest and wildest excitement. Lifting to him, she clung, intoxicated by the exquisite power of his dominant rhythm and the frantic urgency of her own need. The intolerable pleasure reached a crescendo and hurled her into an ecstatic release. She was full of joy and love and gratitude in the aftermath, hugging him close, dabbing kisses on an angular cheekbone, a smooth brown shoulder, indeed any part of him within reach.

'I gather I was good, *yineka mou*…' Resting his angular chin on the heel of one hand, he inspected her with slumberous golden eyes. He rolled back against the pillows and carried her with him, clamping her to his warm, damp body with a possessiveness that turned her heart over inside her.

'I can only compare you and you. But I just think everything's fantastic with you.' By the time she had finished telling him that, her voice had sunk so low with self-consciousness he had to angle his proud dark head down to catch her final words.

'You never will get to compare me with anyone else between the sheets,' Cristos murmured. 'Does that bother you?'

She was delighting in their closeness, thinking back in dismay to the trouble that had been caused when he'd suspected her of hiding out in dark corners with Rory and grateful that she had managed to sort that out. It was a lesson to her, she thought with an inner shiver, a lesson about how easily misunderstandings could occur. Saving face just wasn't worth the risk.

'No…why should it?' she countered softly. 'In fact

I wouldn't be surprised if I fell madly in love with you.'

Lean, strong face hardening, Cristos regarded her with glittering dark eyes. 'Good sex is not love. I found that out as a teenager when the target of my romantic affections invited her best friend to join us in bed.'

Shock shrilled through Betsy. 'Good grief...but *why*?'

'She thought I might be getting bored with just her and decided to surprise me.'

'She was a slut,' Betsy told him in disgust.

'But honest about what she was,' Cristos traded, cool as ice. 'She didn't pretend to love me. I should add that I'm not looking for love from you.'

Long after he slept, Betsy lay awake watching the thread of moonlight that pierced between the curtains dancing across the ceiling. She felt hollow and hurt. She would not be confessing to true love in an effort to get closer to Cristos. Even though they were married, he had rejected that emotional bond most conclusively. In fact the icy note in his rich dark voice had chilled her. Was it possible that he already suspected her feelings for him? Look at the way she had behaved after he had made love to her! She'd been all over him like a rash. Did he found that kind of enthusiasm a big turn-off?

In the morning she wakened alone but a white rose and a jewellery box sat in a prominent position on the pillow beside hers. She pulled back the curtains and opened the box. Sunlight illuminated the creamy perfection of the pearl necklace, which was brought bang up to date with a glittering diamond pendant in the shape of a daisy.

'Wow…' she breathed, fastening it round her neck and pausing only briefly to admire herself.

Hauling on the towelling robe on the back of the bathroom door, she sped off in search of Cristos to thank him. If she lived to be a thousand years old, she would never work the guy out! One minute he was telling her that he wasn't looking for love from her and the next he was giving her a rose and a fabulous necklace to wake up to on the very first day of their married life.

Her bare feet made no sound on the antique rug in the elegant flagstoned hall. She could hear Cristos speaking in his own language and his voice was coming from the room next door to the library. Catching a glimpse of him through the ajar door, she suppressed a loving sigh. Had he been born with a phone in his hand?

'Petrina…' he was saying with low-pitched urgency.

Betsy fell still, her skin turning clammy. She heard every word he said after that but understood nothing because it was all in Greek. What she did grasp was that Cristos sounded concerned and strained and that he was definitely trying to soothe and comfort the woman at the other end of the line. How selfish and blind she had been, Betsy thought then in a sick daze of shock.

All along she had been ridiculously reluctant to contemplate the personal dimension to his broken engagement. She had not even wanted to think about Petrina Rhodias. Why? She had been too jealous. She had never wanted to credit that Cristos might genuinely care for the Greek woman. Now that she was being forced to accept that Cristos did have feelings for the gorgeous blonde, she could finally understand why he didn't want his shotgun bride to love him. He knew that there was not the slightest possibility of his returning her feelings…

CHAPTER EIGHT

ELEGANT in a short sleeveless dress that had a tiny flower print on a yellow background, Betsy came down to breakfast.

'Thanks for the pearls…' she said woodenly, taking a seat at the dining table.

Cristos waited while the manservant tried to attend to her needs before she attended to them on her own account and then dismissed his employee with a nod. 'I think it would be a good idea if you didn't read any newspapers today,' he imparted.

Betsy was no great fan of reading newspapers but in one sentence he had ensured that she would spend the whole of the day perusing the printed word. 'Why?'

'I've always attracted a lot of press coverage. I'm used to it. It doesn't bother me.' Concerned dark golden eyes rested on her delicate profile. 'But you have no experience of how the tabloids sensationalise personalities and events. I don't want you to be distressed.'

Chin at an angle, Betsy was already standing up. 'Where are the newspapers?'

'Betsy—'

'Don't try to tell me that I can't read what's been written about us!' she exclaimed. 'I'm not a little kid!'

'OK…but first I have to explain something about the kidnapping. A member of my own family was behind it,' Cristos delivered grimly.

That did grab her attention. 'You're joking me…a relative of yours?'

'I wish I were joking.' Cristos told her about Spyros Zolottas, who had, she now learned, been one of the men who had died in the helicopter crash with Joe Tyler. 'Unlike my grandfather, I believed that the leopard could change his spots. I was wrong. Spyros decided to use his knowledge of my movements to stage a kidnapping and extract money from Patras. He was with me the first time I saw you. Obviously he realised how he could use my interest in you to his advantage.'

'He's the man you said arranged for me to pick you up that weekend as a surprise,' Betsy recalled.

'To meet you, I was prepared to overlook my security team's concerns and expose myself to a degree of vulnerability that made the kidnapping more likely to succeed.'

'So it was your cousin who was responsible for it all…' For a wordless moment she sat there slowly shaking her head, but deep down inside more turbulent reactions were being born. 'But you're only telling me this now because the newspapers have got a hold of it…am I right? When did you find out that Spyros whatever-you-call-him was behind it all?'

'When I made my first phone call to Patras after we had escaped.'

'But you didn't tell me. We had spent almost a week living together. We were lovers facing the same fears and challenges…and yet you didn't think that I had the right to know *who* had put us on that island?' she demanded shakily, her temper and her hurt rising by equal degrees.

'It was a family matter,' Cristos countered with

measured care. 'When Spyros was killed, my grandfather felt that his family had suffered enough. He saw no advantage and neither did I in publicly exposing Spyros' wife and daughters to the disgrace of his criminal behaviour.'

Betsy was barely listening. Her mind was hopping like a rabbit from mortified peak to peak. 'Was Petrina excluded from the same information?'

'No.'

A bitter laugh fell from her lips. 'That says it all.'

'*Theos mou*…it says what?' Cristos demanded, plunging upright in an expression of mounting frustration.

'Even though I went through that kidnapping with you, I was nobody on your terms. I really was just the silly slapper you seduced to amuse yourself!' Betsy vented painfully.

'That is not how I thought of you…'

'How you behaved tells me exactly how you thought of me!' Tempestuous emotions were pulling at Betsy and a wounded sense of rejection and inadequacy lay at the heart of her agony. 'When I think of how you dared to accuse me of being involved with the kidnappers and all the time one of your own blasted relations had organised the whole thing!'

'I know it looks and sounds bad—'

'And you have never yet apologised for misjudging me!'

'I thought we had gone beyond that level.'

Rising to her feet, Betsy settled furious green eyes on him. 'Where are the newspapers?'

'The library,' Cristos advanced, darkly handsome face taut. 'I won't apologise for believing that it's my duty to protect you from anything that might upset you—'

'Go lock yourself up behind bars, then!'

In the library, Betsy sat down to study the papers. She was shattered to realise that her whole family had come under scrutiny with her. One of her parents' neighbours had used their anonymity to make cruelly cutting comments about Corinne Mitchell. Betsy's eyes filled with tears for she knew how her mother would writhe to see herself castigated in print for all their friends and relatives to see. That Gemma was an unwed mother was also pointed out with a glee that could almost be felt. Stories were angled at presenting Betsy as an ambitious young woman who could only have taken a job as a chauffeur in the hope of meeting and marrying a rich man. Salacious stabs were made as to what must have occurred on the island. Never had she felt more humiliated.

However, at the turn of a page, Betsy learnt that there were still greater depths for her to plummet to in the humiliation stakes. There was more than one two-page spread on Cristos' long and colourful reign as a womaniser.

'I don't want you looking at rubbish like that,' Cristos ground out from behind her.

'I'm sure you don't…' Her tummy churning, Betsy was studying a photo of Cristos getting into a brawl on her behalf at their wedding. She was trying not to feel hideously responsible for what the gossip columnist asserted was a very rare loss of temper for Cristos and 'very revealing of his state of mind on the day he married his pregnant bride'. That was followed by a quote purporting to be direct from Petrina Rhodias in which the Greek heiress referred to Cristos as 'a man of honour shamelessly entrapped by his own decent values'.

'Did Petrina phone you to commiserate with you?' Betsy launched at him, quivering with pain and humiliation.

His jaw line squared. 'What kind of a question is that to ask me?'

'I heard you on the phone to her this morning!'

'As I haven't spoken to Petrina today, that is an impossibility—'

'I heard you *say* her name!' Betsy practically sobbed in her distress.

His ebony brows had pleated and then the light of comprehension flashed through his lustrous dark eyes. 'I did speak to Spyros' eldest daughter before breakfast. She is called…Petrine. Petrina and Petrine. Could you have misheard me?'

Betsy flushed. The difference between the two names was almost indistinguishable and she felt foolish. At the same time she was intensely relieved that she had jumped to the wrong conclusion. 'Yes, obviously I did mishear you,' she conceded almost cheerfully. 'Sorry, my mistake.'

'Spyros' wife and daughters have only just learned that he was responsible for the kidnapping. They are extremely upset and wished to express their regret for what he did to us both.'

'I hope you assured his family that I don't consider them in any way to blame for what happened.'

'Of course. That is generous of you,' he responded approvingly. 'Will you eat some breakfast now?'

'I'm not hungry.' Betsy gathered up the necklace she had removed in a hurried movement. 'I really ought to be ringing Mum and Gemma—'

'Later…' Cristos advised, removing the pearls from her fingers and turning her round so that he could deftly fasten the necklace back into place. 'You've had a rough morning and we're leaving for the airport soon—'

'But it's my fault that poor Mum and Gemma have been lampooned in print along—'

Stunning golden eyes lodged to her, Cristos had pressed a silencing fingertip to her tremulous mouth. 'No, it is *not* your fault. You did nothing to ask for that coverage. Take my advice. Let the dust settle first.'

At his behest she ate a light breakfast.

They were travelling to the airport when she began mulling over what he had said to her earlier. 'What did you mean when you said you hadn't spoken to Petrina Rhodias…*today*?' she suddenly queried.

His brilliant gaze narrowed, superb bone structure taut.

Betsy had lost colour. 'When did you last speak to her?'

'Yesterday. She phoned me before our wedding,' Cristos admitted flatly.

The silence was as taut as elastic stretched to the edge of endurance.

'I've got no right to ask…I know that, but I'm not going to give you a moment's peace until you tell me what she said,' Betsy confided in a driven rush of unsparing honesty.

His devastatingly handsome features set. 'She asked me not to marry you. May we drop the subject now?'

Betsy stared out the window but she was quite unaware of the scenery beyond the tinted glass. So now she knew. On the day of her wedding, Petrina had

waved a come-home-and-all-will-be-forgiven flag.
And why not? Petrina had been engaged to Cristos.
Betsy had been the other woman. Cristos had only
married her because she had fallen pregnant by him.
*A man of honour, shamelessly entrapped by his decent
values.* Since men did not have the ability to conceive
that was rather an unfair assessment, Betsy thought
wretchedly. But was that secretly how he felt as well?

Cristos closed a hand over hers. 'You're my wife
now. Stop dwelling on the past.'

'I can't help it…one minute I'm feeling guilty about
your ex-fiancée and the next I'm feeling sorry for me.'

'I suspect she was the source who tipped off the
press about Spyros having me kidnapped and also
about your pregnancy. Only Petrina knew the score on
both those counts.'

As a device to ease her conscience that revelation
worked; Betsy started feeling a lot less guilty. Had
Petrina Rhodias deliberately set out to destroy their
wedding day? Betsy suppressed a shiver, for such cal-
culated malice was foreign and very threatening to her.
At the same time, however, she was also carefully
thinking over what Cristos had revealed. Clearly, he
had not staged a diplomatic cover-up for Betsy's benefit. He had not gone to Petrina and simply said that
he was sorry but he must break off the engagement
because he was in love with someone else. No, it
seemed that he had told the beautiful blonde the truth
and nothing but the brutal, unlovely truth: that he felt
he had to marry Betsy because she was carrying his
child. Betsy very much wished he had lied.

'We have our whole lives ahead of us, *yineka mou*,'
Cristos drawled, level dark golden eyes resting on her
tense face with a degree of censure. 'Even more im-

portantly, we have the birth of our child to look forward to.'

Her fingers flexed in his. 'Are you really looking forward to the baby?'

His slow, charismatic smile curved his wide, sensual mouth and her mouth ran dry and her heartbeat quickened because he looked so spectacularly attractive. 'Of course I am. I don't care if it's a boy or a girl either.'

Her tension evaporated. She had had so little time to think about the baby. First she had been afraid that she was pregnant, then had come the confirmation and the fear of how she would cope, finally the guilt that she should be happy that Cristos, who didn't love her, should be willing to marry her. Now she found herself wondering whether she would be blessed with a boy or a girl. Whichever, she would be content. In the same way, she swore to herself with determination, she would appreciate what she did have with Cristos rather than brood about what she did not have.

Cristos received a couple of what appeared to be important phone calls soon after the Stephanides private jet landed in Athens. Lean powerful face grave, he settled himself into the limousine beside her and regarded her with veiled dark eyes. 'I'm about to take you back to my home, give you a brief tour and then head straight into the office, *yineka mou*.'

Very much taken aback at the thought of just being abandoned in a strange house in a strange country virtually the minute she had arrived there, Betsy breathed in deep. 'No problem,' she told him, reminding herself that she was not a wimp.

Respect banished the wary aspect from his keenly intelligent gaze. 'As you may have gathered there's no room in my schedule right now for a honeymoon.'

'You never said there would be.' Betsy pinned on a smile, working hard at hiding her disappointment. If anything she felt distinctly foolish for having assumed that he would at least spend a few days with her before he returned to running his business empire. It had become obvious even before the wedding that Cristos worked pretty long hours.

'When I'm less busy, I promise I'll take you away somewhere special and do all that newly married stuff with you.' Cristos was still watching her like a hawk. 'You do realise that you're reacting to all this bad news like a woman in a million.'

'Yes…' Her ready sense of humour sparkled in her green eyes. 'Saintliness is much more likely to induce guilt than recriminations,' she pointed out sweetly.

After a startled pause, he laughed with true appreciation and tugged her across the seat into the strong circle of his arms. After that response she would have braved the Amazon jungle on her own and she snuggled back into him warm with love. A little voice in her subconscious whispered that surely he would have made the effort to find time for a honeymoon with Petrina Rhodias. She jumped on that dangerous inner voice and snuffed it out like a flame threatening a destructive blaze.

His shore-front estate on the Greek mainland took her breath away. She knew Cristos. She had expected an impressive house and was not at all surprised that it overlooked the sea he loved. But she had not been prepared for an historic mansion, the thickly wooded acres of grounds and the private beach or even the two dozen staff lined up to greet her. He made a special point of introducing her to Omphale, an apple-cheeked middle-aged lady with a big cheery smile, who had been his nurse when he was a child.

'Did you tell Omphale I was expecting?' Betsy whispered suspiciously as they crossed a big echoing hall full of light.

Cristos said nothing.

Betsy realised that there was nothing tactful he could say. So many stories about their marriage had appeared in the English newspapers that it was highly unlikely that her condition could still be a secret in Greece. 'It's OK...I'm not being silly—'

'I would have wanted the staff to know anyway, *thespinis mou*,' Cristos confided abruptly. 'How else can they look after you properly? We need to get you signed up with an obstetrician here too. I'll ask around the family for a personal recommendation. It also occurs to me that Greek lessons might be a good idea.'

'I love it when you get bossy...it makes me feel like I'm starring in a madly exciting costume drama where some big tough man talks down to some twittering little woman. Yes, sir, no, sir, three bags full, sir!' For good measure, Betsy raised a hand in what she hoped was a fair stab at an army salute.

Cristos clamped her to him and kissed her breathless. Framing her lovely face with long, spread fingers, he finally drew back from her with pronounced reluctance. His mobile phone was buzzing again.

'I don't need a tour of the house...' Hot pink stained her cheekbones. Almost imperceptibly she was leaning forward, vulnerable green eyes meeting his smouldering appraisal. 'Well...you could show me the bedroom,' she managed, framing that invitation as boldly as she dared.

He groaned out loud. 'I *can't*...don't tempt me.'

He answered his mobile phone, paced away a few feet to speak in low, urgent Greek. He swung back. 'I must go.'

'Trouble at the ranch?' she quipped tightly, striving not to reveal how desperately cut off she felt by his rejection.

He frowned in incomprehension.

'Problems at the office?' she rephrased, feeling very superfluous to his requirements, for he was so obviously mental miles away already.

Stunning golden eyes collided with hers with unexpected force and he laughed and shook his handsome dark head in seeming wonderment. 'No, of course not. What an imagination you have!'

'I'll see you tonight then…'

'It may be late…'

'Then kiss me again,' she heard herself say.

He obliged.

'It may be *very* late,' he confessed when she was holding onto him to stay upright and his own voice had developed a husky edge.

'You'd better kiss me again…to keep me going,' she mumbled.

'If I do it again, it will hurt even more to walk away. You are so beautiful, *yineka mou*.'

'I'll sit up for you,' she promised, watching him back slowly towards the entrance.

Both of them had been so intent on each other that they had not noticed the silver-haired elderly man who was standing there watching them. Cristos cannoned into him and swung round with an exclamation of surprise.

Betsy was welded to the spot. One look at the tall visitor with his spare, sculpted bone structure and deep-set eyes and she knew exactly where Cristos had inherited his good looks from, for the family resemblance was pronounced.

'Betsy…allow me to introduce my grandfather, Patras Stephanides,' Cristos proclaimed with warm pride and affection.

Patras Stephanides walked towards Betsy and stretched out both his hands in an expansive invitation to her. 'Will you forgive a foolish man for his prejudice?' he asked in a voice roughened by emotion.

'Of course.' With a misty smile she grasped his hands and stood while he kissed her with solemn care on either cheek. 'But there's a price,' she warned him. 'There's hours and hours of film on our wedding and I shall make you sit through every minute of it.'

The old man's poker-straight carriage relaxed a little and his appreciative smile lightened his serious expression. 'I shall look forward to my punishment.' He skimmed a wry glance back at his restive grandson. 'Don't let me keep you late, Cristos. I am aware that you are exceptionally busy at present—'

'*Ne*…yes,' Cristos breathed, his attention on Betsy. 'But—'

'A young woman who can tease me within thirty seconds of meeting me is not in the least afraid of me,' Patras quipped with unconcealed approval. 'Stop worrying about your wife. I will look after her. That is what family is for. Good times and bad times must be shared. I'm afraid that for the space of two weeks I forgot that most basic principle.'

Betsy already knew that she was going to like Patras. She always felt most at home with people who were blunt and open in expressing their views. Cristos was more subtle, more sophisticated and much harder to read. His grandfather, on the other hand, was making no bones about his regret at having missed their wedding and his eagerness to heal the breach with his grandson and his bride. She was more than willing to meet the old man halfway. She would have made as much effort even if she had not liked Patras Stephanides. Cristos had been troubled by that breach and for his sake, much more than her own, she was overjoyed that his grandfather had had a change of heart.

'Where do I take you in this house to offer you tea or coffee?' she asked Patras with a rueful grin. 'Cristos didn't get time to show me round.'

'Later, if you will permit me, I will act as guide. I was born here, as was Cristos.' He took her out to a shaded loggia where a slight breeze cooled the air. 'At this hour this is the best place.'

Refreshments were served. Patras answered her questions about the house, which had been in the family for generations. He told her about his collection of classic cars and promised to invite her over to his home for lunch and a tour of inspection.

Just before he departed, Patras studied her with wry acceptance. 'One look was enough to tell me what attracted my grandson to you. You're his Helen of Troy.'

After a startled pause, Betsy laughed. 'Hopefully nobody is about to start a war over me!'

'Don't underestimate Cristos.' Patras looked pensive and rather sombre. 'I'm glad you love him, though. That is as it should be.'

She went bright pink.

The old man awarded her discomfited face an

amused glance. 'I saw how you look at him...it relieved all my concerns.'

Three weeks later, Betsy sat on the top step of the stairs and watched Cristos walk into the dimly lit hall. It was two in the morning.

'And what time of day do you call this to come home?' Betsy enquired with pretend annoyance.

His proud dark head came up, the aura of weariness cast off when he saw her perched on the stairs waiting for him. A softer line eased the hard set of his mouth. 'A time when you should be in bed, Mrs Stephanides.'

Betsy padded down the staircase, a slender figure in a simple white wrap. 'I'm not planning on staying out of bed for very long,' she confided, pink washing her cheeks because she was trying to give him a saucy look of invitation.

He grinned.

'For the baby...' He tossed her the package in his hand.

She unwrapped a brightly coloured toy and a far-away look came into in her eyes: she was imagining a little boy thumping the life out of the drum. It had become a ritual. Every couple of days, Cristos brought back something for the nursery. The drum would join a mobile, a boy toy train set that would require a room of its own, a cute stuffed dog and a little board book that had reminded Cristos of one that he had had as a child.

'Are you hungry?' she asked him.

'I could be tempted...' Dropping a powerful arm round her slight shoulders, Cristos headed her back up the stairs.

Betsy wondered if he was ever going to stop playing

macho man and confide in her. Was he convinced that he had to protect her from all stress simply because she was pregnant? Or was it a Greek male thing? This silent, steely refusal to admit that anything was amiss on the work front? She needed no crystal ball to know that the Stephanides empire was facing challenging times. But Cristos had ignored her every subtle invitation to share his concerns and had denied that there even was a problem.

At the same time he continued to work eighteen-hour days. Only when he was at home after midnight was the phone silent but within a few hours his relentless punishing schedule would begin again. Around eight, his personal staff would arrive to brief him before he even left the house. He would have a working breakfast and walk out to the limousine, dictating orders, listening to bulletins read off sheets. The tension in the air betrayed how serious were the issues at stake and the reality of the crisis.

Crossing the threshold into their bedroom, Cristos rested back against the door, pulled her close and released a low, slow sigh of satisfaction. 'I shouldn't say it…but I love it when you sit up waiting for me. It makes coming home special.'

'That's the point…I aim to make myself indispensable.'

He tipped her head back. His brilliant dark golden eyes inspected her lovely face and the crackling energy of the coppery-red mane flowing round her shoulders. 'You're the most amazing woman…you haven't complained once.'

'I'm running a book,' she teased.

Long fingers knotted slowly into strands of her bright hair. 'I didn't have you picked as the restful, sympathetic type. I underestimated you. I'll never forget how unselfish you've been—'

'Do you think all women are as spoilt and demanding as little kids no matter what the situation?'

'Your predecessors were...' With a slumberous sigh, Cristos bowed his brow down briefly on top of her head and then straightened again. 'I'll go and get a shower.'

The instant he departed, Betsy sped across the vast room to spread wide the French doors and light the candles waiting in readiness out on the balcony. Dragging in the giant floor cushions she had assembled, she tossed a couple of throws over them to create a relaxed atmosphere. Last of all, she brought in the capacious hamper, poured some wine for him and arranged the mouth-watering spread of dishes.

Shedding her wrap, she curled up on the cushions and thought about how ridiculously, incredibly happy she had been since her arrival in Greece. The business emergency that was responsible for forcing Cristos to work such impossible hours had made remarkably little impression on their relationship. But then they had both made a huge effort to make the most out of every minute they could spend together.

There had been early morning swims, midnight barbecues on the beach listening to the surf and snatched snack lunches in his office where sometimes they ditched eating for kissing because they were so desperate to be together. If he had one minute free, he called her and they talked on the phone.

During her very first week in Greece she had been engulfed by the warm and generous hospitality of Cristos' large extended family. There was not a day of the week when she needed to be lonely, for there was always someone wanting to entertain her by taking her out shopping, sightseeing or simply visiting. Perhaps she had learned to appreciate Cristos most when she'd realised just how popular he was with his own relations. For his sake, she had been given the benefit of the doubt and wholeheartedly accepted into his family.

She got on with Patras like a house on fire and he had already developed the habit of dropping in to see her most days. He had assumed responsibility for squiring her about to events where she might have felt a little self-conscious shorn of a male escort. So, she had dined out several evenings in high style and was indeed a little giddy at the amount of socialising she had done.

Cristos emerged from the bathroom, a white towel knotted round his lean hips. Scorching dark golden eyes took in the effect of Betsy, her porcelain perfect skin and stunning shape enhanced by a strappy gold satin nightdress, sprawled among the cushions, and glittered with raw male appreciation. '*Theos mou*…you could seduce a saint with one smile, *thespinis mou.*'

'No saints round here that I know of…'

Cristos groaned. 'Agreed. Are you going to make me eat first?'

Betsy nodded very seriously. 'You know the rules.'

'Do I get a massage later?' Cristos shot her a gleaming look of pure devilment that had the same effect as a megawatt charge on her susceptible heart.

'Forget it,' Betsy advised, her colour heightening, her pride still stinging from the recollection of his response to her very first massage attempt a couple of nights earlier. 'I do not massage people who laugh themselves sick in the middle of my best efforts.'

Eyes bright with unholy amusement, Cristos flung himself down on a cushion opposite and reached for a piece of barbecued chicken. 'It was that very strange New Age music that really sent me off the edge. You do do a very good line in a sexy picnic,' he pointed out in teasing consolation.

She watched him eat. He was truly the most important thing in her world. She wondered how she had ever imagined that she loved Rory because she would not have compromised an inch for Rory or gone out of her way to smooth his path. Whereas Cristos, she just adored, and he might not love her but he did make her feel hugely important to him and hugely appreciated. Around him, she was really beginning to believe that she was a stunningly beautiful, rampantly sexy woman. He told her she was and he made her feel good about herself.

When he had finished eating he reached for her and peeled off the golden scrap of silk and carried her to bed.

'There's just one thing I want to say…about this stuff going on at work that you don't want to talk about,' she framed in a rush.

Superb bone structure tautening, Cristos looked blank. 'What are you referring to?'

'All I wanted to say was…I can live without this big house and all the staff and the luxury—'

'I couldn't,' Cristos slotted in with feeling.

'Yes, you could. At the end of the day, things like that aren't what is most important.'

'Betsy…' Cristos surveyed her with a deeply pained expression. 'I very much appreciate the message that you are trying to give me but there is nothing for you to worry about. I am very wealthy and I have every intention of staying that way, *pethi mou*.'

'But—'

The hard, hungry onslaught of his mouth silenced her. He buried his mouth in the delicate bluish hollow below her collar-bone where a tiny pulse beat and slivers of delicious awareness awakened her body to the animal attraction of his.

'You're so sweet...' Cristos said raggedly, tugging her back against his lean, powerful length to mould the pouting tenderness of her breasts.

The pleasure was a hot and insidious seduction as powerful as an invasion force. She did not and could not resist him. Afterwards, he held her close and murmured her name and she revelled in their closeness.

'Promise me I can meet you for lunch tomorrow. I know dinner's out because you'll be working late but I want to do something to mark my birthday.'

Cristos tensed. 'If I admit I haven't got you anything yet, are you likely to string me up?'

'No...it would be too quick and clean for you. Don't be daft,' she whispered snuggling up to him forgivingly, for when he was frequently so preoccupied he barely knew what day it was she saw no reason why he should have thought to look up her birthday. 'Worry about a pressie next week...tomorrow I just want you and I to get together somewhere other than your office for lunch.'

'I'll arrange it. It's the least you deserve,' he assured her.

The next morning a member of his staff called to inform her that Cristos would meet her at a restaurant at one. Betsy took real care getting dressed up. Her linen dress was the rich colour of amber and the shade looked amazing against her skin and her hair. She was the first to arrive at the restaurant and it was so up-market an establishment that she felt desperately self-conscious seated at her table in what felt like the most prominent spot in the room.

Cristos was late. Surreptitiously, she tried to raise him on his mobile phone but it seemed to be switched off. She rang his office, only to be told that he was out and had not left word of his whereabouts. Believing that he had deliberately chosen to do that so that they could eat without interruptions, she assumed he was already on his way. Time passed painfully slowly. He was late but he would come. For goodness' sake, it was her birthday! She began to rehearse witty but rather stinging comments with which to greet him. She tried his mobile again without success. She did not try his office again because she did not like advertising the reality that she was still sitting waiting for him. It was after two when she left the restaurant, cut to the bone, tears closing up her throat in a painful knot.

The limousine got stuck in traffic. She switched on the television, desperate for something, *anything* to take her mind off her angry, hurt mortification. She was trying to think herself into a more reasonable frame of mind. Presumably some crisis had blown up and he had simply forgotten about her. Was she so self-important she could not accept an oversight?

The news was on, a background buzz in a language she didn't yet understand. She wasn't really looking at it until she saw that it was Cristos on camera. She sat forward then, intent on the screen. He was entering a large modern building, lots of people all around him.

The crowd waiting in the foyer parted and a female figure sped towards him. It was Petrina Rhodias and she flung herself in Cristos's arms. The camera work became positively frenzied, zooming in to show that not a paper width separated the former engaged couple. Petrina looked shockingly beautiful in spite of the tears on her face. She also looked ecstatically happy and Cristos was not fighting her off, imposing a touch of married-man-decent distance or pushing her away.

Betsy hit the off button on the remote control. The car phone was ringing. She stared at it. She just knew it was Cristos calling her but she couldn't face speaking to him. She used the override button on the rear passenger door lock just to climb out into the midst of the bumper-to-bumper traffic and lose herself in the throng of shoppers in the busy street.

Cristos had stood her up on her birthday to stage a public reconciliation with Petrina. A month ago that would have struck her as being as strange as the presence of cameras at the event. She would have been ignorant of how things had once been for Cristos and Petrina. But by asking the right questions of his chattering cousins she had learned a good deal. He and Petrina had once been the leading couple in Athenian high society, two young, beautiful and very rich people from socially and commercially prominent families. Their breakup had been equally big news. The public had once paired the Stephanides heir and the Rhodias heiress like salt and pepper and Betsy had become uncomfortably aware that some people believed that regardless of his marriage Cristos would somehow end up back with Petrina.

Was he back with Petrina? Or was what she had seen on television just a staging post on the path to that ultimate end? How did she know that Cristos had told her the truth three weeks ago when he'd sworn that he had been speaking to Spyros' daughter, Petrine, and not his former fiancée, Petrina? The truth was that Betsy had wanted to believe the explanation he had given her. When you were head over heels in love with a guy, Betsy reflected wretchedly, the last thing you wanted to do was doubt his honesty and his level of commitment.

If she even began to count the number of things that Cristos must have in common with Petrina Rhodias, she would run out of fingers. Petrina appeared to be his perfect match. But they had not been quite Adam and Eve. The fatal flaw had been Petrina's reluctance to attach the strings of fidelity to Cristos. When Betsy had conceived, the perfectly matched couple had been destroyed because Cristos could not bring himself to walk away from his own child.

But before Betsy had married Cristos, she had warned him that she did not want to be his sacrifice. Now her pride was warning her not to make a complete fool of herself. How could she fight to hang onto a guy who didn't love her? If he wanted Petrina back, there was nothing Betsy could do to change that unless she was prepared to use guilt as a weapon to keep him with her. However, she didn't want Cristos on those demeaning terms. What was the point of confronting him about Petrina? Of condemning and crying? She couldn't *make* Cristos love her, could she? Her only option was to surrender with dignity and go back home to London.

Betsy sat on a bench in a busy square striving to talk herself into the dignified option. But there were problems. One, she couldn't bear the idea of Petrina having Cristos. Two, she hated both of them with a vengeful passion that had nothing forgiving or dignified about it. Three, underneath the hatred, she still loved him and walking away from him was easier to think about than actually do.

Tiny shooting pains were tensing her tummy muscles. She had had those same little stabs on a couple of occasions in recent days but, as they had caused her only the most brief and minor discomfort, she had ignored them. She would mention them at her next visit to the obstetrician. A sharper stab made her draw in a surprised breath.

At that point, she emerged from the distancing fog of her unhappy, circuitous thoughts. Fear for her baby seized a hold of her and blanked out everything else. When she stood up the pain got worse and she staggered, doubling over. Suddenly arms came out of nowhere to support her and she registered that she had not contrived to shake off her bodyguards.

'Hospital...' she said jerkily and then she began to pray.

CHAPTER NINE

CRISTOS was waiting to see Betsy when she emerged from surgery.

He looked shattered: ashen pale beneath his bronzed skin, stunning bone structure rigid, gorgeous eyes bleak with shock and regret. Betsy learned that she could hate him almost as much as she loved him for caring to that extent. He had sincerely wanted their child and he was sincerely devastated when she miscarried. But at the end of the day when all the drama was over what was his disappointment and sympathy worth? Not very much, in her opinion. Cristos would have other children…only she was convinced that they would not be with her.

'I don't want to talk about it…I just want to be on my own and sleep,' she told him numbly when he tried to talk to her in her private room.

He closed his lean brown hand over hers, engulfing her smaller fingers. 'Did you see me on the news with Petrina?' he asked tautly.

Betsy yanked her hand free of his in instantaneous rejection.

'I take it that that's a yes. Please listen to what I have to say, *pethi mou*.'

'I don't want to talk to you!' she ground out.

His forceful energy laced the atmosphere. She could feel him willing her to hear him out. 'You have every right to be furious with me and to feel that I've let you down. But things aren't always what they seem—'

164

'Do you really think I care right now? Do you really think that after what's happened I'm sulking about you not turning up for lunch?' Betsy hurled in tempestuous condemnation. 'Why can't you go away and leave me alone?'

'I won't speak. I'll just sit here with you.'

'I want to be on my own,' she reiterated tightly.

'Right now, we should be together. I may not know what to say...I may be afraid of saying the wrong thing, but I do know that I want and need to share this with you,' Cristos drawled with dogged determination.

She turned her back on him to stare at the wall. She could not look anywhere near him without recalling Petrina Rhodias clinging to him as if she had every right in the world to do so. There was a clenched fist inside her where her heart had once been. She wanted to cry but her eyes burned and stayed dry.

'Please just go home and go to bed,' she urged a couple of hours later, unable to bear even his silent presence in the same room for it was a comfort to have him there and she would not surrender to her own weakness. There was no point needing Cristos when he was not going to be part of her life for much longer.

'Don't shut me out like this, *agape mou*,' Cristos breathed in a roughened undertone. 'It's making me feel as though I have lost both of you.'

And he waited and waited with a phenomenal patience that was quite unlike him for some sign of response from her and received nothing. Finally the door slid softly shut on his departure and she wept then, painful noiseless tears that inched down her cheeks like stinging rain. She wept because she loved a truly decent guy, who was still so busy doing what he felt he ought to do for his wife's benefit that he could not yet allow himself to contemplate the fact that there was no longer any reason for their marriage to continue.

When Betsy wakened the next morning, she lay very still and faced how much had changed in the past twenty-four hours. In some respects she was still in shock. She had got so used to being pregnant. Without her even appreciating the fact, the very condition of being pregnant had become a central theme in her life. She had been so careful about what she ate and drank and even more keen to ensure that she took the right amount of exercise and rest. She had read books about pregnancy. She had toured baby shops with enthusiasm, looked at maternity clothes and made plans for decorating a nursery. And now, without warning, all that was at an end. She was no longer an expectant mother and she had not yet come to terms with that cruel reality.

'One of those things,' the obstetrician had told her the day before, giving her statistics that made it clear that early miscarriages were quite common. There was no need for special investigation into the reasons why she had lost her child. Even had she rushed to a doctor when she'd first felt those trifling pangs, she had been assured that it was highly unlikely that anything could have been done to alter the eventual outcome.

Kindly meant platitudes that seemed to take no account of her anguish had followed. She was young. She was healthy. She should try again soon and put this experience behind her. There was absolutely no reason why her next pregnancy shouldn't be successful. It seemed that nobody had the slightest suspicion that in certain circumstances a miscarriage could sound the death knell for a marriage as well.

She had just finished breakfast when Cristos reappeared.

'I saw the tray…you have scarcely eaten enough to keep a bird alive.' He sighed on the threshold, lustrous dark golden eyes sombre and concerned.

'I wasn't hungry. I'll be glad when I can get out of here—'

'If you like you can leave as soon as the doctor has given permission,' Cristos was quick to interpose, his approval of that course unconcealed. 'I'd like to have you home again.'

Suddenly evasive, Betsy bent her bright head. 'I'm not just ready yet,' she muttered hurriedly.

Silence lay while he computed her change of heart.

'You have to let me explain what happened yesterday…and to do it effectively I have to go back a few more weeks in history,' Cristos advanced.

He would give her no peace until she heard him out. She let her head rest back against the banked-up pillows, her hair as vibrant as a fire against the pale linen.

'When I broke off my engagement to Petrina, there was a business as well as a personal dimension to be considered. The Stephanides holdings were on the brink of merging with her father's companies. When we parted, the merger plans went up in smoke. Since then we've been at war in the market-place.'

Betsy was no longer aping relaxation. Stiff with tension, she had sat up. Cristos was telling her that his decision to marry her rather than Petrina had resulted in serious consequences on the business front and she was appalled.

'Why didn't you tell me?'

'What would have been the point? I didn't want you worrying about the situation.'

'That's why you've been working night and day,' Betsy registered with a sinking heart. She was thinking how complex it must have been to pull two such large businesses back from the edge of a merger. By that stage both parties would have been well aware of the strengths and weaknesses of the other and the resulting battle for supremacy would have been even tougher.

'So who's winning?' Betsy enquired tautly.

'I was but it was not a fight I ever wanted. I have a great respect for Petrina's father, Orestes. He is one of my grandfather's oldest friends.'

'Oh, no…is there anything that isn't my fault?' Very pale, Betsy slowly shook her head. She felt so horribly responsible. Nothing but trouble had resulted from her pregnancy. An engagement had been broken and two families and two businesses had been torn apart. Even Patras, it seemed, had suffered as the same divisions affected even his friendship with Orestes Rhodias.

'How is it *your* fault? None of this is your fault!' Cristos exclaimed with fierce feeling. 'I was engaged and playing away. All the responsibility for every wrong thing that has happened since then is mine!'

The sound of such an admission from Cristos twisted like a knife inside Betsy. He had finally got back to basics and acknowledged his own mistake. But what had brought about that miraculous transformation? His loss of Petrina.

'You must not blame yourself for any of this, *yineka mou*,' Cristos asserted with raw conviction. 'It's all over now. Yesterday, Orestes Rhodias had what he believed was a heart attack. I was on the way to meet

you for lunch when I received word that Orestes had
been rushed into hospital. Although we had not been
on good terms, I still wished to pay my respects. I
asked one of my staff to contact you and I'm afraid
the wrong restaurant was contacted…'

It felt to Betsy as though a hundred years had passed
since she had been stood up on that lunch date. 'It
doesn't matter.'

'It matters to me, especially with what happened
afterwards,' Cristos revealed tautly, reluctant to be any
more specific lest he upset her. 'I should have called
you myself. I intended to. I believed I would only be
twenty minutes late.'

'So what happened?' She did not wish to talk about
anything personal.

'Orestes was told that he was suffering from stress
and he was so relieved that his heart was all right that
he made peace with me. The battle between us is at
an end.' Cristos hesitated. 'Petrina arrived at the hospital not knowing whether her father was alive or dead
and she broke down when she discovered that it was
a false alarm…'

'And, of course, you knowing each other so well,
she just naturally fell on you for support,' Betsy filled
in, affecting more interest in her nails than in all the
hugging and so forth that had gone on at that hospital
the day before.

'I didn't like to reject her in front of the television
cameras. She was a bit hysterical,' Cristos proffered.
'There was nothing in it.'

Betsy doubted that Petrina would have looked quite
so ecstatic without encouragement. She had seen him
on camera too and he had not acted as though he were
enduring an attack by a hysterical woman. He had

been smiling that very special smile of his, that smile that Betsy had come to think of as being uniquely hers.

'It's important that you believe that there was nothing personal about her getting all touchy-feely. I haven't looked at Petrina since I married you...'

Literally! He had not had the opportunity. She would not let herself look at him. She felt explosive and bitter and terribly sad. He didn't love her and without love she should never have married him. In particular she should have been careful not to marry a guy who had been engaged to someone else. That had been asking for trouble.

'I don't know you when you're quiet like this...' Cristos confided tautly. 'I'm not used to doing all the talking.'

If she talked she was afraid that she would start crying. She loved him so much. Walking away would be the hardest thing she had ever done and yet, now that there was no longer to be a baby, she owed him his freedom back. He had stood by her just as he'd promised. The costs of doing so, she had just learned, had been even higher than she had realised. Ever since he had married her he had been fighting to keep his business empire afloat. Now thankfully that crisis was over, but it was time for her to move on.

Cristos sank down on the side of her bed and entrapped her restive hands in both of his. Stunning dark golden eyes framed by spiky black lashes assailed hers. 'I want to make everything all right for you again and I can't...I feel helpless,' he confided roughly under his breath.

He seemed so sincere, so caring. She wanted to wrap both arms round him and hug him tight. He was upset about the baby. Was it possible that she had misjudged him? Reacted to an overdose of jealous insecurity?

'I've wrecked so many things in your life,' she muttered shakily.

'That's rubbish.' His hands tightened on hers. 'You haven't wrecked anything.'

Then why did he not mention the possibility of their having another baby? Why the heck could he not offer her the one option that would be a consolation and persuade her that he still saw them as having a marriage that had a future? For goodness' sake, why was she so pathetically weak? All he had to do was be kind and sympathetic and she was willing to keep him tied to her for the rest of his days! Did he deserve that? Did he deserve to have to stay married to a woman he didn't love just because she had fallen inconveniently pregnant? After all, there wasn't going to be a baby now.

Hauling her hands back from his, she flipped away from him, no longer trusting herself that close. 'I need time to think about things—'

'What things?'

'About stuff like how I feel,' she mumbled tearfully.

Cristos gathered her up and crushed her against him. 'You're miserable right now…you shouldn't be thinking about anything!'

She wanted to sneak her arms round him but she wouldn't let herself. He was very good at doing the supportive thing but it wouldn't do to read too much into it. She was in no hurry to remember it but Cristos, she reminded herself, was still the guy who had told her that he wasn't looking for love from her. Pulling herself back together again, she told him she was tired and eventually he took the hint and left. He had only been gone five minutes when the phone by her bed rang.

'This is Petrina Rhodias…may I visit you?'

Betsy tried and failed to swallow. 'When?'

'Now…' The voice was cold, imperious, feminine.

Betsy acceded and wondered whether that had been wise. What could Petrina possibly have to say to her? Was there any point in putting herself through a potentially upsetting meeting? But the truth was that Betsy was curious, very curious about the other woman.

By the time, Petrina entered the room, Betsy was seated in the chair by the bed, clad in a white wrap. Petrina was very much the kind of woman who turned male heads, Betsy noted uneasily. Slim and curvaceous with big blue eyes and a wealth of blonde hair, she was as dainty as an elegant doll.

Petrina studied Betsy with unhidden dislike. 'I won't waste your time or mine. When are you planning to let Cristos have his life back?'

'Meaning?'

'Let him have a divorce.'

'If Cristos wants a divorce he only has to ask,' Betsy countered, tilting up her chin.

'He's not going to request a divorce the instant you lose your baby! Naturally he feels sorry for you.'

Betsy lost colour and compressed her lips.

'Woman to woman,' Petrina said snidely, 'Don't you think Cristos has paid enough yet for the mistake of getting you pregnant?'

Petrina was not a nice person. Betsy felt oddly relieved by that discovery even as she flinched. She wondered if Cristos had ever seen this nasty side of Petrina and knew he would not like it at all. But maybe he loved Petrina. Lovers did not demand perfection. And Petrina had yet to utter any lies. Cristos did feel sorry for his wife and even if he did want a divorce, she too was pretty sure that he would not ask for one while she was still grieving for the child she had lost. Furthermore, Cristos *had* suffered for his decision to marry Betsy. He had suffered both in his business and in his personal life and had even endured differences with his grandfather.

'Have you nothing to say?' Petrina derided, her scorn palpable.

'I just want Cristos to be happy,' Betsy muttered, and she wasn't entirely sure about what she was saying. She believed that she ought to mean every syllable of the sentiment she had uttered. But when it came to picturing Cristos with Petrina, she felt gutted and desperate.

'He will be happy with me. He loves me,' Petrina asserted without hesitation.

'And yet you didn't mind that he wasn't faithful?' Betsy pressed half under her breath.

The Greek woman settled scornful eyes on her. 'Why should it bother me when he amuses himself with a little slut like you?'

Betsy walked over to the door to spread it wide. 'I think it's time you clambered back on your broomstick.'

But, although Petrina departed, Betsy's mind had been made up for her. If Cristos loved Petrina, he deserved the freedom to choose to be with the other woman and Betsy ought to remove herself from his path as tactfully as she could.

'I think I should go home for a while,' she informed Cristos when he came in to visit her that afternoon.

His lean, strong face set in taut lines. 'I don't think that's a good idea at present. You need to convalesce.'

'I can do that in London. I'd like to see my family.'

'Then we'll go together.'

'I'd prefer to go on my own.'

'We've only been married a few weeks,' Cristos reminded her.

'And a very eventful few weeks they've been,' Betsy pointed out tightly.

Cristos lodged at the window and she watched his lean, powerful hands curl into fists and flex loose again. 'I still believe that we should stay together and work through this. We can go away...anywhere in the world that you like, *yineka mou*.'

Her throat thickened and she would not allow herself to meet his intent gaze.

'Will you stay at our country house in England?' he asked abruptly.

'OK.'

'If you are there I can at least be sure that you're being properly looked after.' Suddenly, Cristos sounded as weary as she felt. 'That matters to me.'

'I know...' Her voice was going all wobbly and gruff.

'If I let you go, you have to promise to come back to Greece again.'

Her blood ran cold when she tried to imagine making a final visit to discuss the end of their marriage. 'No problem.'

'I'll give you two weeks—'

'That's not long enough,' she muttered. 'I need a month.'

'A month is a long time,' Cristos gritted.

Yes, long enough for him to tire of the role of being

a supportive husband with no wife around. A month in which they could both heal and he could start considering the futility of resurrecting a marriage in which they were already living apart. When she came back to Greece it would be to agree to the official separation he was almost certain to request. And she would make it easy for him. She would be bright and breezy and he would never ever guess that her heart was breaking...

'I'll phone you every day,' he murmured flatly.

Betsy breathed in slow and deep and suppressed her anguish. 'I think we both need more space than that...I think it would be better if you didn't call.'

CHAPTER TEN

IN THIRTY minutes, the private jet would be landing on Greek soil.

Betsy went off to tidy herself. She wondered if her black shift dress and jacket looked a little funereal. She had put her hair up in an effort to look cool and restrained and now she decided it made her look plain. Cristos might not want her back, but she didn't fancy the idea of him looking at her and wondering what he had ever seen in her.

For the whole month, she had stayed at Ashstead, the Stephanides country house in Devon. The first week she had done nothing but cry and sleep. At the start of the second week she had dutifully gone to London to visit her family, accept their commiserations over her miscarriage and admire Gemma's engagement ring. When she returned to Devon, she began going out for long country walks. Her appetite came back and a sparkle returned to her eyes. Patras came to stay for two days and, although she had to ban him from trying to behave like a heavy-handed marriage guidance counsellor, she really enjoyed his company and absolutely adored all the stories he told her about Cristos as a boy. By the end of the fourth week, when Cristos had his PA call her to relay her travel arrangements, she was feeling thoroughly rested.

But while she had come to terms with her grief, she found it quite impossible to come to terms with the prospect of losing Cristos. Even worse the concept of surrendering Cristos to Petrina, who she was convinced was wholly undeserving of him, kept her awake at night. She missed him every hour of every day. A hundred times over, she almost lifted the phone to ring him just to hear the sound of his voice. Only the question of how she would explain herself prevented her from succumbing to temptation.

After the jet landed at Athens, Betsy was ferried across the airport to board a helicopter. When the flight winged out across the Aegean Sea she wondered where on earth she was being taken, yet in another sense she didn't care enough to try and ask. If journey's end meant politely accepting that her marriage was over, she would just as soon remain an eternal traveller. As she'd left London her spirits had been buoyed up by the knowledge that she would soon be seeing Cristos again. Fear of what he would be telling her had plunged her into the downward descent of misery.

So preoccupied was she that when the helicopter landed she scrambled out without the smallest idea of where she was. A few hundred feet away the turquoise sea shimmered in the late afternoon sunlight and the golden beach bore not a single footprint. Disbelieving the evidence of her own eyes, she discounted the strong sense of recognition that was trying to persuade her that she was back on the island of Mos again. In that mood, she hurried round the helicopter and there, nestling below the headland, sat the little villa with the terracotta roof.

Kicking off her shoes, which were sinking into the sand, and discarding her jacket, Betsy sped on towards the house. A figure appeared in the doorway and her steps faltered and started to slow. Shock slivered through her: it *was* Cristos. Sheathed in tailored beige chinos and a black shirt, he looked drop-dead gorgeous. He stayed where he was, waiting for her to come to him. To a woman starved of the sight of him, he was the equivalent of a feast after a famine.

Several feet from him, Betsy froze in her tracks. She was bewildered by the shock of finding herself back on the island and she hated the fact that she'd been taken by surprise. 'What is this set-up? What on earth is going on?'

'You're going to be angry with me,' Cristos imparted.

'Don't tell me what you think I'm going to do…tell me why I would be angry.' Suddenly she stalked forward and pushed past him to peer indoors with suspicious eyes. 'Do you have Petrina in there?' she demanded.

His astonishment was unfeigned. 'Is that a joke? Petrina wouldn't dream of gracing a place as primitive as this with her presence.'

Still very much on the defensive, Betsy folded her arms. 'I don't think it's primitive but I do think it's extremely tasteless to bring me back here.'

The deafening roar of the helicopter taking off again drowned out all possible exchanges for a couple of minutes. Betsy threw her bright head back and pursed her lush mouth. 'How am I supposed to get back to Athens?'

'You're not…at least not without me,' Cristos informed her. 'I'm afraid you've been kidnapped for the second time in your life.'

'Kidnapped?' Betsy parroted.

'When you and I were last here, things were very

simple. I thought it would be a good idea to take our marriage back to basics too.'

Betsy could not believe her ears. 'Are you telling me…that you lured me out here with the intention of keeping me on this island against my will?'

Cristos nodded.

Betsy had fallen very still. 'To save our marriage?'

'I appreciate that it would be more ideal if I gave you a choice, but I want the chance to do some tough negotiating and if you can't walk away from the table, it gives me an advantage.'

'True…on the other hand, I might not want to walk away,' Betsy pointed out a little unevenly. 'Hasn't that occurred to you?'

'That's not how you've been behaving. No visits, no phone calls, an enforced separation,' he reminded her bleakly.

Betsy stopped hiding behind her pride. 'I didn't want you to stay with me just because we were married. I wanted to give you the chance to choose…and I really did think that you might choose Petrina.'

'Even after all you and I have been to each other?' Cristos framed in apparent amazement.

'She told me you loved her—'

'You've met Petrina…but *when*?' Cristos demanded, taken aback.

Betsy explained about the visit she had received at the hospital.

Cristos swore under his breath in his own language. '*Theos mou*…if I had known I would not have been responsible for my actions. How could she be that cruel? You had only just lost our child. You were so vulnerable then.' His clear dark golden eyes were bitterly angry. 'There was no love in my relationship with her—respect, familiarity, and tolerance perhaps. I thought that that was all there was. I honestly believed I wasn't missing anything…and then I met you.'

And then I met you! Betsy savoured that admission, for, if Petrina had only qualified for respect and tolerance, he was making it sound as though Betsy herself had made much more of an impression. He had never loved Petrina. The relief of learning that fact made her feel dizzy. He had set her worst fear to rest.

'Everything got so complicated with you.' Cristos raked long fingers through his cropped black hair. 'You told me you loved Rory. When I saw you together at our wedding, I believed you *still* loved him—'

'No…no!' Words of eager disagreement tumbled from Betsy. She closed her hands over his. 'I grew out of Rory a long time before I even realised it. That's all over and done with—'

Rueful golden eyes flared over her anxious face. 'I was so angry and jealous on our wedding day that I almost wrecked our marriage before it even began!'

'But you said you believed me when I explained about Rory.'

'Wasn't that also the evening that you gave me multiple-choice answers on that subject?'

At that reminder, Betsy reddened. 'It's been a very long time since I thought I loved him. I was trying to save face. You put me on the spot but you weren't giving me any answers about how you felt about Petrina,' she reminded him. 'I needed reassurance too.'

'Once I knew you were pregnant, I didn't have to think about how I felt about you,' Cristos acknowledged, tugging her gently indoors and out of the strong sunlight that he could see was making her uncomfortable. 'I knew I wanted to marry you. I didn't have a moment's doubt. It was that simple—'

'But it wasn't simple for me,' she protested.

'It was only simple for me because I loved you. I didn't appreciate it then, but that was *why* marrying you was such a simple decision for me.'

'You love me...' Betsy blinked in bemusement, not certain she was hearing him right. 'When did you decide you loved me?'

'At our wedding. I saw you with Rory and I wanted to rip him apart. But I realised that if I didn't want to lose you, I would have to try and pretend that I hadn't seen anything that bothered me.' His dark eyes momentarily reflected the bleakness of that recollection. 'That was a major challenge, *pethi mou*. But it was also the moment when I appreciated that there was virtually nothing I would not do to keep you and that I loved you.'

Betsy's eyes were stinging like mad. 'You love me...honestly?'

His slow, devastating smile slashed his darkly handsome features. 'Do you think I'd kidnap just anybody?'

Betsy surprised both herself and him by bursting into floods of tears.

In consternation, Cristos hauled her into his arms. '*Theos mou*...what's wrong? What did I say?'

'You said you loved me...and I've been so miserable the last few weeks and I needn't have been!' she sobbed helplessly.

He bent down and swept her off her feet to carry her into the air-conditioned cool of the bedroom. 'The last month has been hell for me too,' he admitted rawly, 'but I didn't want to be unreasonable and crowd you. I wanted to be with you but you didn't seem to want to be with me—'

'That's not how I felt. But we only got married because I'd fallen pregnant,' Betsy reminded him jaggedly, her breath catching in her throat. 'When I lost the baby, I thought there was no reason for you to want to stay with me any more and that our marriage was over—'

'You crazy woman...how could you have been so blind?' Cristos demanded incredulously. 'We were really happy together. It was insane. I was living through the most stressful time of my entire life at the office and coming home to paradise with you. I've never been so happy in my life...in fact I didn't know it was possible for one person to make such a difference. Yes, it was devastating when you had the miscarriage but we still had each other—'

'But we *didn't*...I went back to England. You're probably going to find it hard to believe but I love you too!' Betsy gasped apologetically.

Cristos vented a startled laugh and shook his handsome dark head in amazement. 'Patras said no woman could be interested in hearing what a smart-mouthed kid I had been unless she loved me. I didn't believe him.'

'He was right...he had me hanging on his every word. When he came to stay, I was just missing you so much...' Betsy squeezed out tearfully.

'You love me!' Without warning Cristos lifted her up in the air like a doll and spun her round and back against him.

'Oh, that was so uncool...' Betsy whispered with

immense appreciation, stretching up to frame his face with her spread fingers and survey him with loving pleasure. 'But now I finally believe you're mine.'

His stunning dark golden eyes clung to hers. 'Always, *agape mou.*'

'So what happened to that…you weren't looking for me to love you stuff?' Betsy enquired saucily.

'That was my pride talking.'

She wound her arms round his neck and pushed into the hard, muscular heat of his big, powerful body. He answered her encouragement by kissing her breathless. Crushing her to him, he muttered thickly, 'I'd love it if we tried for another baby some time—'

Inspired by a project that had such immediate appeal to her own heart, Betsy leant back from him to say, 'Would right now be too soon?'

The strain etched in his lean, powerful face evaporated. 'I was afraid that I was going to upset you and that maybe you wouldn't want to risk a second pregnancy—'

'We just had bad luck. Oh, I do wish that you'd told me how you felt when I was in hospital,' Betsy admitted unsteadily, her emotions very close to the surface.

'That I'd like us to try again? One of my female cousins warned me on no account to mention anything like that in case you felt I wasn't showing proper respect for the child we had just lost,' Cristos confided in a taut undertone. 'I didn't want to risk hurting you.'

'I wouldn't have felt like that…I was just desperate for some sign from you that you still saw us and our marriage as having a future,' Betsy explained.

'Our future is together, *pethi mou.* I went through hell when you went back to England,' Cristos admitted raggedly, gazing down at her with adoring intensity. 'Never again do I want to go through the agony of wondering if I've lost you—'

'From now on, you won't have that worry,' Betsy assured him with sunny good humour and newly learned confidence. 'You won't even get time off for good behaviour.'

Cristos threw back his handsome dark head and laughed with true appreciation. 'I love you,' he intoned then with smouldering intensity and she dragged him down to her and found his sensual mouth for herself.

Almost a year later, Betsy gave birth to their daughter, Karisa. Karisa was followed eighteen months afterwards by the arrival of a son, Darian.

Overjoyed with his two great-grandchildren, Patras Stephanides bought the island of Mos and gave it to Cristos and Betsy to mark their fourth wedding anniversary.

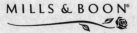

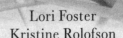